G.R. Dampier

Monograph on the Brass and Copper Wares

of the North-Western provinces and Oudh

G.R. Dampier

Monograph on the Brass and Copper Wares
of the North-Western provinces and Oudh

ISBN/EAN: 9783337387037

Printed in Europe, USA, Canada, Australia, Japan

Cover: Foto ©Andreas Hilbeck / pixelio.de

More available books at **www.hansebooks.com**

A MONOGRAPH

ON THE

Brass and Copper Wares

OF THE

NORTH-WESTERN PROVINCES AND OUDH.

BY

G. R. DAMPIER, C.S.

Published by Authority.

ALLAHABAD:

Printed at the North-Western Provinces and Oudh Government Press.

1891.

PREFACE.

The following report has been prepared in accordance with G. O. No. $\frac{2199}{I—133}$ dated 2nd August 1893, and Government of India letter No. $\frac{41}{238}$, dated 5th July 1893.

Under these orders, a list of questions bearing on the subject of the Copper and Brass Manufacture of these Provinces was drawn up and despatched to each district. A special officer in each district was deputed to write a district report on the lines indicated in the form of questions circulated, and these reports were submitted to me when completed. Partly from these reports, and partly from personal inquiries instituted at Mirzapur, which is itself an important centre of the trade, I have been enabled to compile the Provincial Monograph on the Brass and Copper Manufactures of the North-West Provinces and Oudh.

Of the reports received from the various districts, that submitted from Benares, compiled by Mr. J. F. Fanthome, Deputy Collector, gave me the greatest assistance. The report was admirably drawn up, and was full of copious information, both as regards the actual manufacturing processes and also as to the present economic conditions of the Brass Trade in Benares. After this I may mention the Etáwah report, drawn up by Mr. H. R. C. Dobbs, C.S., the Bareilly report, drawn up by Pandit Janardhan Dat Joshi, the Agra report, drawn up by Mr. H. Hoare, C.S., and the Farukhabad report, drawn up by Saiyid Muhammad Ali, as having been, each in their own department, of special use in compiling this monograph. The Mainpuri and Moradabad reports were also good. My best thanks are due to Mr. Crooke, Magistrate and Collector of Saháranpur, for the hints he has given me as to the form which this report should take, and for the valuable advice I have derived from him during its compilation.

Sahdranpur.   G. R. DAMPIER, C.S.

INDEX.

A

MONOGRAPH ON THE BRASS AND COPPER WARES

OF THE

NORTH-WESTERN PROVINCES AND OUDH.

—o—

CHAPTER I.

Section 1.—The origin of the use of brass and copper in India for vessels of domestic or other use is a subject too obscure to admit of discussion in this report. Mention is made of them as far back as the oldest books reach, and they must have existed for years previous to the writing of these records. Still, though it is difficult to imagine the ordinary native of India bereft of his '*bartan*,' there must have been a time when he only used clay or wooden pots and pans. Judging from the present existing primitive communities, such as the jungle tribes of Africa, &c., the gradation of materials used for culinary and other utensils would seem to be unbaked clay, wood, baked clay; then, as the arts of civilization improve and manufactures develop, metal, such as brass and copper and sometimes gold and silver, till at last the higher stage of glass and china is reached. The metal stage is always of long duration; owing to its superior stability, metal cannot give way before china and glass till these commodities can be so cheaply produced as to render their comparative fragility a matter of little importance. Europe itself has only just emerged from the metal stage; half a century ago pewter drinking pots and metal plates were common articles of use; now-a-days, with the exception of a few inns and colleges, where the genuine article is still kept up, and some hotels, where imitations are used, the foaming pewter has almost disappeared in England.

Origin of vessels of domestic use.

India is still in the metal stage and is likely to remain there long. Putting aside the comparative dearness of European glass, &c., the Hindu prejudices, in connection with cooking and eating vessels, which will be treated of in the succeeding sections, must long prove an insuperable barrier to the general adoption of glass and china ware.

Section 2.—Considering the very large part that brass and copper vessels play in the ordinary daily life of the Hindus and Muhammadans, the rules that refer to them in the scriptures of either religion are extremely scanty. We have the following commandments enjoined in the 5th chapter of the Code of Manu:—

Rules concerning their use in Hindu and Muhammadan scriptures.

(1) Metallic vessels, such as golden, gem and stone vessels can be cleaned by ashes, water and earth.

(2) Gold, shell, pearl, stone and engraved vessels of silver can be made pure simply by washing. As gold and silver are produced by the combination of fire and water, they can best be cleaned by the thing to which they owe their origin.

(3) Copper, iron, bell-metal, brass, pewter and lead pots can be purified by alkali (*reh*), tamarind and water according to their quality.

In the Dharmshastra Achardarsha Pirgam, eating from copper vessels and keeping milk or curds in them is forbidden, and nothing edible is to be kept in brass vessels. In general, according to the Hindu Shastras, gold and copper pots are held to be of first class purity; next to these come vessels of silver and brass; and lastly, those made of bell-metal. Vessels made of iron are considered impure, and it is believed that wherever they are used, gods and the spirits of deceased ancestors have no access. Turning from Hinduism to Islám, we find the information on the proper use of metal vessels no less meagre. The Durr-i-Mukhtar, an authority on Muhammadan customs, contains the following precepts :—

"It is detestable to eat in brass and copper vessels. Earthen vessels are better and more excellent, for the Prophet of God has said that those who keep these vessels in their houses are visited with respect by angels."

"It is not detestable to eat in tin, lead, crystal or cornelian vessels."

"It is lawful to eat out of vessels which are set, studded or embroidered with silver."

"The use of gilded vessels is right according to all authorities . . . . for the gilding cannot be separated, and is only a colour, which is of no consequence."

Such are the precepts of either creed : the following section will show how far they are carried out into practice.

Section 3.—Nothing could be more typical of the crudities of the Hindu Shastra system than the beliefs engendered by the rules above quoted anent the use and disuse of vessels of certain metals. As we have seen, the Hindus divide their vessels into pure (sudh) and impure (asudh). Now under the latter head are classed alloys in general, and *phúl* or bell-metal in particular. The use of *phúl* is hedged about with a number of minute ceremonial injunctions. A *phúl* tray becomes impure if a man of a lower caste than the owner eats out of it or if a man of different religion touches it ; nay, more than this, it is generally held that *phúl* vessels become impure anyhow by use, so that every member of the family, as far as circumstances permit, has his separate pots made of this metal. Some husbands even will not allow their wives to eat from the *phúl tháli* in which they themselves are wont to take their food. In fact, *phúl* vessels are regarded in the same light as earthen vessels, and should they by any mischance become impure, it is not sufficient to cleanse them in the ordinary way ; they must be taken back to the brassfounder and remoulded. And yet these *phúl* vessels are the only sanitary vessels that the Hindu possesses, excluding, of course, earthen vessels. Milk or curds, if kept in a brass vessel, go bad, and similarly anything acid cannot be cooked in a vessel of that metal. For all these purposes *phúl* pots have to be used. Consequently we have this curious result, that the best cooking pot that the Hindu possesses is under the ban of the most vexatious ceremonial restrictions. The impurity of *phúl* is due to its being an alloy and containing (*rángá*) pewter—an impure metal. Hindus believe that a god presides over each metal, and the names of these correspond with those from which the days of the week take their name. The sun presides over copper ; the moon (Soma) over silver ; Mangal over brass ; Budh over lead ; Brihaspati over gold ; Sukra over pewter ; Sani over iron ; and Ráhu over *kánsí* (a copper and zinc alloy).

Broadly stated, the difference between the use of metal vessels by Hindus and Muhammadans, is that Hindus use brass and alloy vessels, while Muhammadans only use copper vessels. The use of copper vessels by Hindus is prohibited, as we have seen, by the Shastras, nominally on account of the sanctity of the metal, though very possibly, as is so often the case in ancient ceremonial codes, a sanitary reason underlies the religious sanction imposed.

In the Durr-i-Mukhtar, cited above, section 2, the use of both brass and copper vessels for eating purposes is prohibited to the faithful. The prohibition against the first named metal is still strictly observed, brass being held *makrúh* (detestable) by all good Muslims, but the prohibition against copper has been evaded. The Durr-i-Mukhtar approves the use of tin eating vessels. Muhammadans therefore use copper vessels, but are careful to have them *tinned*, thus at once providing themselves with sanitary cooking ware, and obeying the letter, if not the spirit, of the traditions of their Prophet.

To the general rule given above that Hindus use brass and alloy vessels, while Muhammadans only use copper, there are several important exceptions.

The Gujratis use all copper vessels except a brass *lotá*, which they use for the offices of nature. The Borás, a sub-caste of Khatris, who are very numerous in Benares, use copper vessels for all domestic purposes. The Saksena Kayasths of the Doab and western districts cook their meat and other food in tinned copper *patílís*.

Popular prejudices and beliefs concerning them.

On the other hand, among poor and ignorant Muhammadans living in isolated villages in the Dehát it is no uncommon thing to find brass *thális* and *lotás*, &c., employed where we should expect *agane* and *badhnás* in more civilised localities.

Section 4.—There are several points of interest in the method of using vessels among Hindus and Muhammadans that call for some note.

Their general use.

In an ordinary Hindu household the cleaning of the vessels is usually done by the housewife herself, who performs the *rôle* at once of cook and scullion. In well-to-do houses a female servant, usually either of the Kahár, Hajjám or Bárí caste, is kept for this purpose and receives from Rs. 3 to Rs. 5 per mensem. The vessels are cleaned with ashes, sand or clay and some kind of straw or grass such as *khas*, *munj*, *puthawar*, or *bánkus*. This cleaning of vessels is technically termed *chauki bartan*.

In well-to-do Muhammadan households a khidmatgar is kept for the same purpose, who cleans the vessels with hot or cold water. But besides this daily cleansing, the vessels used by Muhammadans have to be tinned from time to time. The intervals at which tinning is necessary are as follows :—

Vessels exposed twice a day to fire in cooking ... 15 days to 1 month.

,, ,, ,, ,, ... 1 month to 2 months.

,, in constant use, but not exposed to fire... 1 month to 1½ months.

,, seldom used, and ,, ... 2 months to 3 months.

The ordinary price for small vessels is 2 pice per vessel or annas 10 per score, but there are special rates for larger vessels.

At marriage ceremonies among Muhammadan and high caste Hindus it is customary to ask the loan of dishes, *pándáns*, *gulábpásh*, &c., and other articles necessary for a stylish entertainment from rich friends. Among Hindus each man contributes some of his vessels, but neither Muhammadan nor Hindu ordinarily ever hires any vessels for the occasion. The only approach to this is the large *deg*, holding 50 gallons, which Muhammadans hire from the Bhatiárs or professional cook on such occasion. In the middle Hindu castes, such as Kayasths, &c., the Chaudhri or headman of the community keeps a supply of spare vessels, which he purchases from the proceeds of fines imposed by the caste *panchayats*, and lends them out to persons requiring the use of them. In Benares the hire of a large *deg* capable of holding 20 sers of rice is 4 annas each ; of a *kafgir*, *seni*, or plate, one anna each per diem. The professional bakers (*wánbái*) keep a supply of such vessels always in hand, and they often make a living by the hire of them. The substitution of vessels of other ware for vessels of brass and copper make is comparatively rare. Poor Muhammadans will use baked clay vessels when they cannot get other, but Hindus, however poor, will rarely use clay vessels, owing to the fact that, as above stated in section 3, Chapter I, a clay vessel once eaten out of becomes impure in a Hindu's eyes and has to be rebaked before it can be used again. The poor Hindu will generally use a platter of leaves (*dauna*) when he is unable to afford more noble ware. Nor is adoption of English, china, and glass ware proceeding rapidly. Hindus owing to religious scruples will not use it, and Muhammadans, as a rule, cannot afford such fragile luxuries. Still, in the houses of the richer Musalman it is not uncommon to find English glasses in use. The standard of comfort will have to rise very much before any general adoption of English glass and china ware takes place.

The pawnbrokers drive a thriving trade in brass vessels. Pawning his pots and pans is the resource of the indigent native when hard put to. As might be expected, the interest payable is very high. The vessel is pawned at the rate of 8 annas per ser, and interest on the debt accrues at the rate of 3 to 6 pice in the rupee per month. These are the Benares rates ; variations occur of course all over the Province.

The custom of having some distinguishing mark on the family plate, which obtains so largely in Europe, hardly can be said to be at all general in these Provinces. Sometimes proprietors have their names rudely scratched on the vessels, but further than this, they do not seem to go.

Section 5.—We will now proceed to describe some of the commonest vessels in use among Hindus and Muhammadans of the present day.

The lota. The badhná.

The *lota* is perhaps the first of the numerous pots and pans in use among Hindus that the newcomer to India learns to recognise. There is scarcely any Hindu so poor that he does not own a *lota*. It is a *multum in parvo*, serving at once the purpose of glass, cooking pot, and toilet service. It is generally cast in *phúl* or beaten out in brass. The shape of the *lota* appears to have altered somewhat. Formerly it was angular and somewhat thicker than it is made nowadays. Both of these qualities were, however, open to objection—the former on the score of cleanliness, the latter on the score of expense. The tendency has been therefore to round off the corners and lighten the weight. I am indebted to Pandit Janardan Joshi, Deputy Collector of Bareilly, for the following account of the points of a good *lota*:—

(1) All the parts of a *lota* should be freely accessible to the fingers as to admit of its being cleansed with earth. Hence it should have no angles and should not be too deep.

(2) A man should be able to hold it with his fingers just pressing on the brim. Hence in spite of condition No. (1) the mouth of the *lota* should not be too wide.

(3) It should be cheap, graceful, and durable.

The modern Nagpúri *lota* coming from Mirzapur satisfies all these conditions and is rapidly becoming very popular. I believe that not less than 60 per cent. of the *lotas* in every district belong to this class. It is prepared by the casting process and is displacing all other *lotas* in India. The upper half is polished and the lower half left rough.

The *badhná* also known as the *Lota Tontidár*, *i.e.*, *Lota* with a spout (*Tonti*), is the Muhammadan counterpart of the *lota* and serves the same purposes with the exception that I do not think it is ever used for cooking. The *badhná* is beaten out of copper, tinned, and is shaped much like a teapot, having a spout and lid. Some very ornamental *badhnás* are made at Lucknow. The following explanation of the preferences shown by Muhammadans for a spouted *lota* is given in one report : " The Quran ordains that a man shall perform his ablutions in running water. Muhammadans use therefore for this purpose a *lota* with a spout to it, as the water when poured out of the spout is considered to be running within the meaning of Scripture."

The price of a *badhná* varies from 15 annas to Re. 1-4 per ser. The price of a *lota* depends on the metal of which it is made ; a brass *lota* sells from 13 annas to one rupee eight annas per ser, a kaskut *lota* from 12 annas to one rupee per ser, a phul *lota* from one rupee six annas to one rupee eight annas per ser.

Section 6.—The *katorá* is a small vessel, used alike by Muhammadans and Hindus. The Muhammadan *katorá* is almost exactly like an ordinary English cup, with no handle. It is made of thin sheet copper, tinned, and varies in price from a few annas upwards ; the price increasing with the weight of metal used. The Muhammadans generally keep a number of small cheap *katorás* of the above description, for entertainments at the Id-ul-Fitr and other festive occasions. The Hindu *katorá* is a thick shallow saucer, made of *kaskut*, *phúl*, or brass by casting and is generally used for cooking vegetables, the Muhammadan *katorá* being chiefly employed as a drinking cup. Though I have distinguished between Hindu and Muhammadan *katorás*, it is no uncommon thing to find a Musalmán using a brass or *kaskut* Hindu *katorá* which has undergone the indispensable tinning process. As a rule, the lower castes of each community are very lax on these points.

Katorá.

The price of a *katorá* varies a good deal. The small thin Muhammadan type can be bought for a few annas. The heavier Hindu *katorá* made of *phúl*, &c., generally costs a rupee or more.

Section 7.—The *batuá* is the cooking vessel, *par excellence*, of the Hindus. It is round shaped, with a narrow, flat brim and no length of neck. In it are cooked rice, *dúl*, and vegetables. The *batuá* is made of brass, bell-metal, and *kaskut* : those made of bell-metal are preferred, as it is quite safe to cook acid substances in them, but they are more expensive than those made of brass and *kaskut*. The *batuí* is a small edition of the above. Natives of slender means generally prefer two

Batná, Degchis, Patili.

batuís to one *batuá;* for if they have two *batuís*, they can cook the rice in one and the *dál* in the other, both at the same time, instead of first having to cook the rice and then let that get cold while they prepare the *dál*.

The *degchi* and *patíli* are kindred vessels to the *batuá*, that is to say, they are used almost entirely for cooking purposes. They are of quite a different shape to the *batuá*, being flatter and more angular. The *degchi* is of course a vessel of purely Muhammadan origin, and the *patíli* is generally regarded as a Muhammadan vessel, though both one and the other when made of brass or alloy are freely used by the meat-eating castes of Hindus to cook their food in.

Copper *degchis* and *patílis* are the Muhammadan cooking vessels; they are made in the same shape as the brass *degchi* and *patíli* and are tinned. The copper *degchi* is, however, such a very familiar article that no lengthy description of its merits or demerits is necessary.

In the hills they have a *degchi* of peculiar shape, termed a *tauli*. The shoulder of this vessel is sharp and square, and not rounded off as in the corresponding "plains" vessel: the slope from the head to the shoulder is straight and not bulging; the part below the shoulder too is rather shallower than in the "plains degchi." The *batuá* is almost invariably cast: the brass *degchi* and *patíli* are both cast and beaten out: the copper degchi and *patíli* are only beaten out.

The prices of these vessels vary a good deal according to the metal of which they are made. Brass *batuás* run from 11 annas to 13 annas per ser: *kaskut batuás* 11 annas to 12 annas per ser: *phúl* batuas from one rupee to one rupee six annas per ser. Brass *degchis* cost from 12 annas to 13 annas per ser :ₚphúl *degchis* from one rupee to one rupee four annas per ser: copper *degchis* from one rupee one anna to one rupee two annas per ser. *Kaskut patílis* sell from 12 annas to 14 annas per ser: phúl *patílis* from one rupee four annas to one rupee six annas per ser: copper *patílis* sell at one rupee per ser. It must be understood that these rates are continually fluctuating with the market rate of raw metal.

The average life of a *batuá*, *degchi*, or *patíli* varies considerably with the status of its owners. If he is a rich man and has several meals a day, the *batuá* may last him any time from two to five years; if he is poor and his meals few and far between, his vessel, be it *degchi, batuá*, or *patíli*, will last considerably longer.

Section 8.—The *thálí* or tray, made either of beaten brass or more rarely from *phúl* or *kaskut*, is a very common article of every day use and there are few Hindu households that do not number one or more of these vessels on the list of their ordinary culinary utensils. *Thálís* vary much in shape and size and ornamentation, but it is with the plain and homely tray that this section deals. Such trays are bought at prices varying from 12 to 14 annas a ser if made of brass, and Re. 1-5-0 per ser if made of *phúl*. The *parát* is a larger kind of tray and is more generally to be found in well-to-do houses. The *tasla* is a smaller and quite plain and is usually found in the houses of the poor. The *lagan* is the Musalmán counterpart of the *thálí*, and is made of copper. The *rikábi*, also a Musalmán vessel and made of copper, is rather a plate than a tray, though it belongs to the *thálí* or tray class. Both *lagan* and *rikábi* sell at about Re. 1 per ser.

The thálí, lagan, rikábí, parát, tasla.

Section 9.—This extraordinary misnomer, as one of my correspondents terms it, can only be said to have a title to its present name on the score of shape, not of material. It is an obvious copy of an English half pint tumbler in brass, alloy, copper. When it first came into use, is impossible to find out, but it has now become such a recognised article of domestic use that uneducated natives regard it as a purely native vessel. The same differentiation of custom between Hindus and Muhammadans with regard to it is observable, *i.e.*, the Hindu's " glass " is made always of brass or alloy, and the Muhammadan's "glass" of tinned copper.

The gilás (glass).

The price of a " glass " depends not only on the metal of which it is made, but also on the degree of ornamentation applied to it. Its general price is about Re. 1 per ser.

Section 10.—In concluding this chapter it may be as well to give some idea of the amount, quality, and value of the utensils found in the houses of the poor and rich. It must, however, be premised that the following lists are mere approximations, as it is impossible to lay down any hard and fast rule as to the amount of vessels which a native may possess. If a native of small means is asked how many vessels he possesses, he will generally astonish the enquirer by going through a list of vessels that appears completely out of proportion to his rank of life. On further enquiry it will generally be found that the majority of superfluous vessels he mentions are the general property of the family, his own stock being limited to two or three culinary utensils of prime necessity.

In a poor peasant's house the list of brass vessels to be met with would naturally be small. Probably we should find the following :—

If *Hindu*—

1(*a*).

Name of vessel.	Description.	Metal.
(1) Thálí or thala or parát ...	A tray	Brass.
(2) Batná	Cooking pot	Kashut.
(3) Lotá	Small water pot	Brass, phúl.

The approximate value of these would be about Rs. 3.

If *Musalmán*—

1(*b*).

Name of vessel.	Description.	Metal.
Lagan	Tray	Copper.
Patíl or degchí ...	Cooking pot ...	"
Badhná	Water pot with spout ...	"

Estimated value Rs. 3-8 to Rs. 4. In addition to the above, a small zamíndár would have the following :—

If *Hindu*—

2(*a*).

Name of vessel.	Description.	Metal.
Katorá	Saucer	Phúl or kashut.
Glás	Glass	Phúl.
Kalchhal	Spoon	Brass.
Gagra	Large water-pot, for drawing water.	Copper.

The actual value of these vessels would be about Rs. 9 or perhaps less. Adding on, however, the vessels in 1(*a*) and allowing for the fact that a zamíndár would probably have several lotas and katoras, we may estimate the total value of his utensils at from Rs. 14 to Rs. 15.

If *Musalmán*—

2(*b*).

Name of vessel.	Description.	Metal.
Saní	Large and generally ornamental tray.	Copper.
Katorá	Saucer-shaped or cup-shaped vessel.	Phúl or copper.
Kafgír	Spoon	Copper.
Rikábí	Plate	"
Ábkhara or a gláss ...	Drinking glass ...	Copper or phúl.
Sarposh	Cover for the degchi ...	Copper.

The actual value of these would be about Rs. 7, but adding on the articles mentioned in list 1 (b) and remembering these are often held in duplicate, we may estimate the total value at Rs. 14 to Rs. 15.

A rich Hindu mahájan or a Muhammadan gentleman in affluent circumstances not only holds a larger quantity and better quality of all the vessels previously enumerated, but has also a number of other articles of use and luxury. Articles of pure luxury, and those used on ceremonious occasions, do not differ with the creed of their owner, as is the case with the lower species of utensil: hence separate lists of these are unnecessary.

Vessels possessed by a rich mahájan, &c.

• *Rich Mahájan—*

Name.			Description of vessel.			Metal.
Chhalal	...	...	Sieve	...	...	Brass.
Hawla	...	...	Large vessel for holding water			"
Katordan	...	...	Vessel for holding food	...		Phúl.
Majha	...	...	" " water	...		Copper.
Jharna	...	...	Perforated spoon			Brass.
Gangal	...	...	Vessel for holding water	...		Copper.
Sánsi	...	...	Small tongs	...	...	Brass.
Dhol	...	...	Water bucket	...	...	"

Rich Mussalmán—

Name.			Description of vessel.			Metal.
Deg	...	...	Large cooking pot	...		Copper.
Chamcha	...	...	Spoon	...	...	"
Tabaq	...	...	A plate	...	...	"
Mahetaras	...	...	A spit	...	...	"
Tashtari	...	...	A small salver or plate	...		"
Tasht	...	...	} A platter or large salver	...		"
Rikábi	...	...				

Besides these vessels, rich Muhammadan and Hindu *rúíses* generally possess a number of the following articles :—

Name.			Description of vessel.			Metal.
Áftábá	...	...	Small wash hand basin	...		Brass.
Chilamchi	...	...	" "	...		"
Silafchi	...	...				
Pikdán	...	...	} Spittoon	...	...	Brass and other metals.
Ugaldán	...	...				
Husndán	...	...				
Khásdán	...	...	} Pán box	...	...	Copper, brass.
Pándán	...	...				
Patilsou	...	...	Candle stick	...	...	Brass.
Chírághdán	...	...	} Lamp stand	...	...	"
Chaughara	...	...				
Pichkárí	...	...	Vessel to hold rose water	...		Copper and alloy.
Ittardán	...	...				
Gulábpásh	...	...	} Rose water sprinkler	...		Copper, alloy, but generally of silver.
Datnklá	...	...				
Kali	...	...	} Huqqa stand	...	...	Alloy, silver-plated.
Farshi	...	...				

It is almost impossible to give even an approximate estimate of the value of the vessels possessed by a rich Hindu or Musalmán. Supposing all the vessels above enumerated to be made of copper or brass or some alloy, and that there are more than one of each kind of vessel, we should not be far wrong in putting the total value of the vessels between Rs. 150 to Rs. 300. If of course, as is generally the case, in the houses of any rich *rátses*, the articles used in ceremonious entertainments, such as *gulábpásh* and *pándán*, are made of silver, the total value of the vessels would be considerably more.

Section 11.— Vessels of brass and copper are largely employed in the worship in the temples of Hindus, but their number, shape, and design differ somewhat according to the sect to whom the temple belongs. The following list shows approximately the vessels usually found in a Saiva or Vaishnava temple:—

Sacrificial vessels.

(1) *Ghanta*, a bell, usually made of *kaskut* or *phul*.
(2) *Arti*, a lamp.
(3) *Dhúpdáni*, censer.
(4) *Katori*, saucer, generally three in number:—

    (a) *Ark*, for keeping *chandan* or sandal.
    (b) *Pádá*, for keeping rice.
    (c) *Achwan*, for keeping *til*.

(5) *Digdáni*, a small box, used to hold the materials (*ghi* and cotton) for the *arti*.
(6) *Singhásan*, a seat for the idol.
(7) *Pánchpátr*, a vessel for holding water.
(8) *Achmani*, a small spoon used with the *panchpátr* for making drink offering.
(9) *Arghá*, a narrow boat-shaped vessel, invariably of copper, used for making offerings to the *pitri*.
(10) *Tháli*, a plate for flower offerings.
(11) *Rikábi*, a plate in which fruit and sweetmeats (*bhog*) are offered to the god.
(12) *Dibia*, a vessel, in which the *hom* or burnt sacrifice is made.
(13) *Chhatra*, the umbrella held over the god.
(14) *Jhánjh*, a pair of cymbals, clashed at the time of the offering.

All these vessels are usually made of copper, which metal, as has been mentioned in section 3, is held most sacred by the Hindus. Many of them may be, and often are, made of brass, while in the richer temples of Benares silver and gold are often employed in their manufacture. It may be interesting to note some differences between the Saiva and Vaishnava use. The bell or *ghanta* used by Saivas is known as the *Nandi ghanta* or bull-bell, from its bearing the figure of *Nandi* or the bull, sacred to Mahadeva; whereas the bell used by Vaishnavas bears the figure of a *gárúda* (a mythical bird or vulture, half man, half bird, on which Vishnu rides—now identified with the crane) and is termed the *gárúda-ghanta*.

The *Singhásan*, used for seating Siva, has a pyramidal canopy over it, called the *Sirdlá*, while Vishnú's *Singhásan* is quite open.

The *achmani* or *pánchpátr* used in the Vaishnava worship, bears the figure of Ganesh or Hanumán marked on it, while that used by a *Saiva* will have a cobra (*nágphan*) on it or a *nandi*, and will be moreover *ashtadhátaka*, or compounded of eight metal and made in the *Sirálá* shape.

The requirements of a Jain temple are very different from those of a Vaishnava or Saiva place of worship, and of a much more simple character. Only three metal vessels are used:—

(1) *Dhúp*, a censer.
(2) *Dip*, a *ghi* lamp.
(3) *Náibedh*, a small dish in which food and sweatmeats are offered to the god.

Vessels of worship used in Hindu temples are cleaned either by a Brahman or Kahár. As they are mostly of copper, earth, &c., is not used for cleaning them, but lemon juice or some other similar acid. It is believed that acids clean untinned copper better than anything else.

CHAPTER II.

Section 1.—In India every trade or occupation is nominally supposed to be carried on by a particular caste, who in general take their name from the business to which they belong. The brass and copper manufactures are no exception to this rule. Theoretically the trade, whether of making and retailing brass and copper vessels, is entirely in the hands of the Kaseras and Thatheras, the hereditary brass and copper workers, who will be fully dealt with in the succeeding section. Theoretically this is so ; practically, as has already happened in nearly every purely occupational caste, a number of outside men from other castes have come in and taken up a business not strictly theirs. A glance at the list of castes employed in the brass ware trade is instructive : nearly all castes are represented, from the twice-born Brahman to that social outcaste—the Bhangi. That a Lohár or Sunár should leave his own particular metal and engage in the manufacture of brass and copper goods is not astonishing, but that Kunbis, a purely agricultural caste, or that Kalwárs, whose ordinary business is to distil and retail liquor, should adopt this trade, is very surprising. Still more extraordinary is the callousness that permits a Bhangi at Benares to manufacture idols and sacrificial implements—a good example of the inconsistency of modern Hinduism.

Castes employed in the brass trade.

This development of the brass trade among workers of alien castes can be accounted for only by two reasons ; either the business is so lucrative that the scruples of caste have to go by the wall as is not unfrequently the case, or—and this I imagine to be the true reason that—the pressure of population is so intense nowadays in India, the struggle for life so hard, that amid the general weakening of caste principles by education and European ideas, men of whatever caste will betake themselves to any trade that will furnish them with their daily necessities. Annexed to this section is a table showing the various castes employed in the districts as given in the District Report. From this it will been seen that, setting aside Kaseras or Thatheras, who are to be found in every district, save the hill districts, where they are replaced by the Dom-Tamota, alien castes are found employed in the brass trade in the following order of frequency :—

> Banya in seven districts,
> Lohár in six districts,
> Sunár in five districts,
> Ahír in two districts,

while single instances of alien castes employed in the brass trade are to be met with in Benares and other districts.

Name of district.	Name of caste.	Name of district.	Name of caste.
Saháranpur ...	Thathera. Kasera. Sunár.	Furukhabad ...	Various, but not Muhammadans.
Muzaffarnagar ...	Thathera.	Mainpuri ...	Thathera. Lohrá. Lodha.
Meerut ...	" Kasera. Lohár Ojhá. Mewati.	Etáwah ...	Kasera.
Aligarh ...	Thathera.	Etah ...	Banya. Kasera. Thathera.
Muttra ...	"	Bareilly ...	" Kasera.
Agra ...	Lohár. Thakur. Barhai. Paraha.	Bijnor ...	Thathera. Kasera.
		Moradabad ...	Generally by Muhammadans.

Name of district.	Name of caste.	Name of district.	Name of caste.
Sháhjahánpur .. {	Kasera. Thathera.	Ballia ...	Kasera.
Cawnpore ...	"	Gorakhpur ... {	Thathera. Kasera.
Fatehpur ...	"	Lucknow ... {	Thathera. Kasera.
Hamírpur ... {	Kasera. Sunár.		Thathera. Kasera. Sunár.
Allahabad ... {	Thathera. Lohár. Purabia. Banya. Kurmi.	Unao ... {	Ahír. Halwai.
		Rae Bareli ... {	Thathera. Kasera.
Benares ... {	Thathera. Kasera. Lohár. Banya Rastogi. " Agarwála. " Kasarwáni. " Kasaundha. Sarógi Banya. Ummar " Kandú. Kosri. Chhatri. Sunár. Bangáli. Khatri. Kalwár. Brahman. Kumhár. Gond. Gowin. Patwa. Musalmán. Luniya. Marhatta. Niglágar. Kanchan Rámjani. Chhipi. Kayasth. Teli. Halwai. Bari. Dhanje. Hajjám. Ahír. Bhangi. Christian.	Saltánpur ... {	Thathera. Kasera. Lohár. Sunár.
		Hardoi ... {	Thathera. Kasera.
		Kheri ...	Thathera.
		Fyzabad ... {	Kasera. " Banya.
		Gonda ... {	Thathera. Kasera. Purabia. Banya.
		Bahraich ... {	Thathera. Kasera. Kándú Banya.
		Sultánpur ... }	Kasera. Thathera.
		Partábgarh ...	Kasera.
		Bara Banki ... {	Thathera. Purabia. Banya.
		Naini Tal ... {	Kasera. Thathera.
		Almora ...	Dom-Tamota.
Mirzapur ... {	Thathera. Kasera. Ahír.	Garhwál ...	"

Section 2.—In nearly every manufacturing town the bulk of the manufacture is carried on by two castes, Kaseras and Thatheras. The exact difference between these two castes is not easy to determine, as nearly every district gives a different explanation of the matter. As regards the names, Kasera is derived from *kansá*, the alloy out of which women's ornaments are chiefly made, and Thathera from *táshta-kará*, meaning a polisher.

Difference between Kasera and Thathera.

Mr. Crooke, in his Ethnographical Handbook to the North-Western Provinces and Oudh, gives Kasera as the maker of brass vessels and Thathera as the seller, and, according to Mr. Ibbetson, the same difference obtains in the Panjáb. The majority of the reports I have received favour an interpretation just the reverse, namely, they make Kasera the capitalist dealer and Thathera the artizan. This agrees with the explanation given by Mr. Johnstone in his Brass Report for the Panjáb. Besides this definition of the artizan and dealer, we get a number of other classifications. Thatheras are said to only make cast vessels, while Kaseras produce the beaten work. This is opposed by Nesfield, who states that Kaseras do the moulding, while the polishing and engraving is carried on by the Thathera. Again, a frequent classification met with in the reports is that Thatheras make useful metal utensils, while Kaseras only make women's ornaments, out of *kínsá*. This sounds plausible enough, but unfortunately at Benares just the reverse of this is the case. There and in one or two other districts it is the Thathers who manufactures female ornaments.

In view of these glaring contradictions that meet us at every step, it is impossible to lay down a very hard and fast line of demarcation. Both castes are becoming to a large extent purely occupational, and in many districts the terms Thathera and Kasera are now used as synonymous. Judging from the reports alone that I have received, I should be inclined to favour the classification of Kasera as capitalist dealer and Thathera as skilled artizan.

Section 3.—At the last Census the total number of Kaseras in North-Western Provinces and Oudh was 7,273. Nearly all these are returned as inhabitants
Statistics of distribution. of the Eastern Divisions of Benares and Gorakhpur, eleven hundred odd are returned for Oudh, while the Agra Division is returned as possessing but three female Kaseras, and in the Meerut and Rohilkhand Divisions Kaseras are conspicuous by their absence. These figures conflict with the reports sent in on the subject of the brass, Kaseras being reported in many districts in which, according to the Census, they do not exist. Of Thatheras the total number at the last Census was 20,823. They are returned for almost every district in the province. This return of Thatheras alone for many districts where it is known Kaseras exist, goes far to show what little distinction really exists in the native mind between them.

Section 4.—The economic conditions under which the trade is carried on vary much from district to district. In large towns they approximate more and
The wages and profits of the brass trade. more to European methods, while in small towns and villages the industry has barely emerged from the state where the handicraftsman is workman, master, producer, and retailer all in one. In Benares, Mirzapur, Aligarh, Moradabad, Agra, and other important cities, differentiation of labour has taken place ; not, indeed, to that machine-like degree to which it is carried in English factories, but still to such a point that each separate process is allowed to claim the undivided attention of a separate workman, who bears a name indicative of the special kind of work in which he is engaged and who receives pay proportionate to the value of his department as compared with that of the other departments of the whole industry. These large factories will employ up to twenty or more men and be owned by some rich capitalist Banya or Kasera, who supplies his employés with tools, &c., after the European fashion and pays them on the scale mentioned further on in this section.

In small towns we meet quite another state of affairs. Often a single family supplies all the workmen necessary for its factory, father and sons working together and, if necessary, should there be any extra work to be done, hiring one or two day labourers at two annas a day to help them in the *unskilled* portions of their craft. The working employer is an economic advance on this primitive state. Though himself not disdaining to help at polishing a *thálí* or casting a *lota*, he has in his employ two skilled artizans and one or two day labourers to do the bulk of the work. He pays the former from four annas a day and the latter two annas a day, while for economic purposes his own wages might be reckoned at Rs. 9 or Rs. 10 per mensem. So by slow stages the advance goes on till we reach the point where perfect division betwixt department and department of the industry takes place and master and employé become so utterly separated that the whole western gamut of wages, expenses, and profits once more meets our view.

The following is a list of the operatives ordinarily employed in a factory :—

Native name.	Description of work.	Remuneration.
Dháiá ... Khulwá ... Sánchiá ... Bhariá ...	The man who pours the molten metal into the mould from the crucible.	From 2½ annas per day in the eastern district to 8 annas per day in Agra.
Chhilaiya ... Kharádi ... Koniá ... Kunwá ...	The man who works the lathe	From 3 to 6 annas per day.
Khinchiá ... Charkhkash ...	The man who pulls the lathe	From 2½ to 3½ annas per day.
Khál Phénké ... Dhaunkié ...	The man who works the bellows.	Three annas per day.
Bitié ...	The men who works the file	From 2½ to 3½ annas per day.
Pitalyé ... Gharalyé ...	The man who hammers out sheet brass.	Up to 8 annas per day.
Ghanwá ...	The man who beats out native cast plates with a sledge hammer.	Up to 6 annas a day.
Pabárá ...	The man who holds the plates while being beaten.	Up to 4 annas a day.
Saachewálá ...	Moulder	2½ to 4 annas per day, unless working by contract.

The foregoing list fairly represents the ordinary constitution of a factory, in which no ornamental work is done. But besides these we find in larger factories, where differentiation of employment has been carried to a higher point, a further addition :—

Native name.	Description of work.	Remuneration.
Lakriwálá ...	The man who supplies wood to the furnace.	
Leojera ...	The man who looks after metal while it is being fused.	As average of Rs. 7 per mensem.
Pandikárché ...	The man who cleans the crucible	
Gulliwálá ...	The man who looks after the native cast plates.	
Beldár ...	An odd-job man... ...	Three annas per diem.

Skilled artizans command much higher wages, and can often dictate their own terms to their masters. They are paid not by the day, but by the ser of metal, on which they work their skill. In Moradabad, the graver, known there as *nlch.iyá*, gets only from Rs. 5 to Rs. 10 per month, and the colourer or *rangkharia* from Rs. 7 to Rs. 10. At Benares the *naqqásh* or chaser receives for ordinary vessels, such as cast *lotus*, 1½ annas per seer, but for more elaborate work he receives a higher rate according to the quality of the work required of, or turned out by, him, the wage paid amounting sometimes to as much as Rs. 2-3 or more per ser. Similarly the *Dháliá's* wage depends entirely on what he is called upon to cast. In ornamental work he receives as much as 12 annas per ser.

There is no obligatory apprenticeship in India as used to exist in England in the time of the trade guilds, nor does it even seem to have existed, as there is no word at all that expresses the idea. Juvenile apprentices are, however, employed in most large factories, especially those in which ornamental work is carried on. These earn from eight annas a month, according to their age and abilities. Women are apparently never employed in any branch of the copper and brass ware industry. Nor is this to be regretted; the work is very hard and the condition under which much of it is performed not very healthy, so that the employment of women in this trade might exercise a bad influence on the *physique* of the coming generation.

It is excessively difficult to gauge accurately the profits of any Indian trade. Centuries of misgovernment have rendered the Indian merchant so suspicious that he imagines any Government inquiry into the state and circumstances of his trade can have but one object —the assessment of a new tax on his industry, or the enhancement of one already existing; consequently he either grossly understates his profits, or gives such misleading statistics to work upon, that no result of any much practical importance can be deduced therefrom. The reports themselves that have been submitted from the various districts are evidence of this. For instance, in Mainpuri the profits of an average manufacture are estimated at from Rs. 50 to Rs. 150 per annum. In Muzaffarnagar, a place of less importance as regards the brass trade, they are estimated at Rs. 800 per annum. Allowing for carelessness in appraisement or in observation, we still have a divergence so considerable as to discredit in part, if not entirely, the data from which these results have been obtained. It is not an easy matter to work out the profits even of a manufacturer: the price of fuel and of raw metals is continually fluctuating, while as regards the very considerable income derived by many manufacturers from the mending up and repairing of old vessels, we have absolutely no data whereby to gauge its extent. Taking, however, an average of the returns from the small manufacturing towns, such as Saháranpur, Rao Bareli, Sitapur, Mathura, &c., the ordinary profits of the manufacturer appear to be about Rs. 200 per annum or possibly a little more. Ordinarily, the manufacturer does not send his goods directly to the public, but they pass through the hands of a middleman. The profits of the retailer are even more hard to ascertain than those of the manufacturer. In Rae Bareli, Mr. Norrie states, they make a profit of one anna in the rupee, or about 6 per cent. on their sales, but is of opinion, in which I concur, that their profits are considerably higher than this. Taking again an average of the profits reported from the various districts, and excluding one or two preposterously high figures, we get the ordinary takings of a retail dealer in the smaller towns to be from about Rs. 250 to Rs. 300 per annum.

In Benares and other large manufacturing towns it is common to find the business of manufacturing and retailing combined in the hands of some large firm. The profits of such firms are sometimes very large. The following extract from the Benares Report, based on the Income Tax returns, will give some notion of the takings of these large industrial proprietors:—

"Of the 613 stalls or factories in Benares, there are 33 businesses of which the annual profits are large enough to be assessed to income tax. The profits range from Rs. 500 to Rs. 3,000 and average Rs. 1,006 to each firm. The total profits amount to Rs. 33,212, assessed at Rs. 642. There are 25 firms between Rs. 500 and Rs. 1,000 profits; five between Rs. 1,000 and Rs. 2,000; and three between Rs. 2,000 and Rs. 4,000 profit. The largest business is one with profits amounting to Rs. 3,700 a year and is owned by a Rastaugi Banya."

Section 5.—The following table, prepared by the Land Records Office, shows the imports of brass and copper for the years 1890-91, 1891-92, and 1892-93 :—

From where imported.	Brass unwrought.			Brass wrought.			Copper unwrought.			Copper wrought.		
	1890-91.	1891-92.	1892-93.	1890-91.	891-92.	1892-93.	1890-91.	1891-92.	1892-93.	1890-91.	1891-92.	1892-93.
	Mds.	Mds.	Mds.	Mds.	Mds.	Mds.	Mds.	Mds.	Mds.	Mds.	Mds.	Mds.
From Calcutta ...	8,576	4,877	5,100	4,001	4,420	7,129	28,539	37,590	36,765	2,590	4,204	1,909
„ Bombay ...	30,475	35,843	43,441	973	2,084	1,927	19,520	16,586	19,880	3,513	2,706	2,851
„ Other places ...	3,584	1,044	2,860	9,076	11,228	13,402	521	1,169	1,475	1,274	1,063	1,931
Total ...	41,684	41,364	46,416	14,050	17,737	22,456	49,280	55,945	58,140	8,196	8,568	6,711

No statistics are to hand as to the account of tin and zinc imported for the purpose of alloying, though the consumption must be considerable. It is evident from inspection of the above statements that while almost all the brass is imported from Bombay, the lion's share of the copper comes up from Calcutta. It is rather difficult to account for this, as the difference in weight between the metal and the alloy is not sufficient to make shortness of railway transit any object. The only explanation appears to be that brass is chiefly imported from England, between which and the port of Bombay there are numerous lines of steamers and cargo boats running. Copper, however, is not only imported from England, but from many other countries which trade chiefly with Calcutta and not with Bombay. Hence the bulk of the copper is imported into Calcutta instead of Bombay.

And exports. A comparison. **Section 6.**—The following table shows the chief places to which wrought and unwrought brass and copper were exported in the years 1890-91, 1891-92, and 1892-93 :—

Statement II showing exports of Copper and Brass from North-Western Provinces and Oudh to other Provinces during the years 1890-91 to 1892-93.

To where exported.	Brass unwrought.			Brass wrought.			Copper unwrought.			Copper wrought.		
	1890-91.	1891-92.	1892-93.	1890-91.	1891-92.	1892-93.	1890-91.	1891-92.	1892-93.	1890-91.	1891-92.	1892-93.
	Mds.	Mds.	Mds.	Mds.	Mds.	Mds.	Mds.	Mds.	Mds.	Mds.	Mds.	Mds.
To Madras Presidency, excluding Madras port.	...	4	8	121	29	58	...	...	...	19	4	8
" Bombay Presidency, excluding Bombay port.	...	...	...	1,028	719	629	...	...	...	123	65	39
" Sindh	...	12	...	376	386	263	...	...	...	52	111	61
" Bengal, excluding Calcutta port	72	38	41	15,631	15,917	16,740	723	23	217	794	293	308
" Panjáb	404	765	944	8,412	9,538	9,237	1,556	1,053	670	2,452	3,287	1,556
" Central Provinces	77	6	18	6,030	6,016	7,909	9	3	7	388	379	319
" Berar	...	1	...	1,633	967	825	...	...	1	37	65	68
" Rájpootána and Central India	134	62	91	7,175	8,264	7,609	504	9	6	626	682	580
" Nizam's Territory	...	...	...	7	10	11	...	...	...	38	77	46
" Mysore	...	...	...	10	9	4	...	...	...	...	...	...
" Madras port	1	...	...	24	21	58	...	...	...	8	...	34
" Bombay "	16	...	...	616	678	1,059	...	...	...	109	86	62
" Karachi "	...	...	...	3	1	2	...	...	...	...	...	...
" Calcutta "	11	...	2	6,123	4,920	5,577	2	10	...	257	198	189
Total	715	885	1,097	46,978	54,065	49,910	2,565	1,006	901	4,883	5,249	3,555

A comparison between this statement and that of imports in section 5 shows us that for the year 1892-93 the imports of wrought and unwrought brass exceeded the exports by 19,667 maunds. The export of wrought brass was very high, exceeding in fact the total weight of the raw material imported by over 1,000 maunds and leaving only some 13,000 maunds of wrought brass for the consumption of the province. This of course would be quite insufficient for the wants of the swarming population of this province. The deficiency is made up from home manufactured brass, i.e., that which is alloyed in these provinces. In the statistics of copper wrought and unwrought the imports exceed the exports by 60,395 maunds. Now with the exception of a few sacrificial vessels and one or two water pots, pure copper vessels are not used by Hindus; Muhammadans are numerically too small a community to absorb this mass of copper. Therefore it must go to form the alloys from which the vessels of Hindus are chiefly made and thus explain the anomaly, suggested by the statistics of brass import and export, that 13,000 maunds of brass suffice for a Hindu population of 40,380,168.

Section 7.—It is very difficult to obtain satisfactory statistics of the internal movements of brass and copper ware within the province. The table given below affords some notion of the large traffic there must be from district to district, but owing to metals being usually lumped up under one head in municipal accounts, some details, such as to the comparative demand for alloys other than brass, are not forthcoming. From the table, however, it is obvious how Hindu Benares almost monopolizes the brass export trade to the other districts, while her copper trade is a very unimportant affair. It is curious Allahabad being returned as such a large exporting centre. This must be due to its position as a large junction, since the actual brass and copper manufacture carried on at Allahabad itself is of no commercial value. Railways have enormously deleveped the export and import trade between the large centres of manufacture. This branch of the trade is chiefly in the hands of Banyas, who also undertake the work of distributing the produce of the large manufacturing cities to all the small towns and hamlets of the interior of the various districts.

Internal movements of the trade.

Statement *III, showing imports and exports of Copper and Brass within*

Article	From whence exported.	Imports into the								
		To Meerut Division.			To Agra Division.			To Allahabad Division.		
		1890-91.	1891-92.	1892-93.	1890-91.	1891-92.	1892-93.	1890-91.	1891-92.	1892-93.
Brass, unwrought	Meerut Division ...	...	...	...	35	42	340	...	4	—
	Agra ,, ...	197	148	77	...	...	...	476	8	...
	Allahabad ,, ...	6	20	...	252	304	26	...	...	...
	Benares ,, ...	245	155	153	22	28	10	1,554	870	2,547
	Rohilkhand Division ...	...	6	...	17	—	...	...	2	—
	Oudh ,, ...	...	...	...	...	...	...	...	14	...
	Total, Brass unwrought ...	447	324	225	326	374	375	2,330	893	2,547
Brass, wrought	Meerut Division ...	...	...	...	1,563	3,530	3,714	606	1,091	1,296
	Agra ,, ...	2,100	2,760	3,070	...	...	...	3,090	2,356	2,583
	Allahabad ,, ...	745	73	56	1,563	1,676	2,527	...	...	...
	Benares ,, ...	4,339	4,876	5,015	1,941	2,230	2,609	11,389	15,944	15,944
	Rohilkhand Division ...	702	1,110	1,363	274	105	251	154	470	499
	Oudh ,, ...	34	32	15	21	50	26	144	190	86
	Total, Brass wrought ...	8,060	8,852	9,130	5,366	6,671	7,927	14,384	20,051	20,348
Copper unwrought	Meerut Division ...	...	...	...	11	6	82	...	—	1
	Agra ,, ...	101	38	35	...	...	...	21	26	25
	Allahabad ,, ...	21	78	...	439	57	82	...	...	...
	Benares ,, ...	5	105	...	7	...	...	8	...	18
	Rohilkhand Division ...	76	...	...	1	...	...	...	...	...
	Oudh ,, ...	397	323	...	5	5	...	...	...	...
	Total, Copper unwrought ...	597	424	35	468	68	64	22	20	54
Copper, wrought	Meerut Division ...	...	...	...	74	64	140	23	34	7
	Agra ,, ...	379	606	458	...	...	...	236	202	302
	Allahabad ,, ...	47	71	4	66	86	124	...	...	...
	Benares ,, ...	33	105	1	28	37	42	62	45	38
	Rohilkhand Division ...	43	141	17	11	5	18	55	47	7
	Oudh ,, ...	307	425	11	60	97	47	164	216	133
	Total, Copper wrought ...	809	1,350	471	239	289	371	560	544	487

North-Western Provinces and Oudh during the years 1890-91 to 1892-93.

NORTH-WESTERN PROVINCES AND OUDH.

To Benares Division.			To Rohilkhand Division.			To Oudh.			Total.		
1890-91.	1891-92.	1892-93.	1890-91.	1891-92.	1892-93.	1890-91.	1891-92.	1892-93.	1890-91.	1891-92.	1892-93.
6	...	...	59	126	21	...	4	...	100	176	261
...	...	18	91	106	13	...	4	8	764	256	176
207	260	11	...	24	...	127	127	...	1,091	735	85
...	...	...	...	...	4	1,226	1,320	2,487	3,347	3,383	5,326
63	...	...	...	...	...	...	850	408	80	858	408
190	144	81	...	327	860	...	...	...	196	485	941
972	404	110	150	583	809	1,353	1,815	2,903	5,578	4,303	6,965
80	36	27	2,733	3,505	4,824	30	63	99	6,963	7,217	8,900
80	59	53	2,422	3,840	4,081	391	523	201	7,190	9,538	10,296
2,933	2,596	2,723	610	723	470	59,70	8,019	9,462	11,825	13,387	15,044
...	...	...	2,096	775	2,967	7,429	6,307	6,634	27,309	30,094	35,169
63	68	53	...	...	...	200	277	675	1,386	2,520	3,062
373	651	490	127	257	746	...	...	...	704	1,190	1,372
3,470	3,720	3,353	8,001	9,100	13,094	14,084	15,851	19,971	53,364	64,245	73,523
...	...	49	170	219	14	14	...	...	195	225	96
4	...	...	260	204	76	1	20	34	387	273	150
843	26	130	41	41	25	152	20	...	1,023	226	297
...	...	...	...	3	2	26	32	101	50	140	122
...	...	...	...	...	...	...	25	56	74	26	58
69	21	235	...	34	57	...	...	...	470	283	305
414	47	427	471	501	174	233	107	103	2,201	1,173	947
43	...	...	101	116	64	10	14	11	251	223	222
22	43	16	319	263	369	64	184	182	1,040	1,306	1,387
450	210	940	130	105	96	896	790	1,076	1,579	1,277	2,262
...	...	...	82	16	9	531	124	111	486	337	201
5	...	...	...	...	...	73	83	197	196	226	329
412	240	210	60	53	208	...	...	...	1,003	1,061	669
932	499	1,106	642	568	825	1,362	1,153	1,579	4,545	4,423	4,900

Section 8.—The chief centres of brass and copper work in the North-Western Provinces and
Oudh are Benares, Moradabad, Lucknow, Mirzapur, Agra, and

Chief centres of Brass Trade. perhaps Farukhabad. Each is to a certain extent representative
of a particular branch of the trade, and though Benares, by reason
of the magnitude of its manufactures and the world-wide fame it has achieved, seems to dwarf all
other competitors, yet in their own particular line Moradabad and Lucknow are quite able to hold
their own. Benares and Mirzapur may be said to be the centre of ornamental and useful Hindu
brass and copper work, while Moradabad, Lucknow, and Farukhabad fulfil the same purpose for
the Musalmán section of the community. Agra is unrepresentative and of late appears to have
been devoting itself to the reproduction or adaptation of vessels and articles of European shape and
type. It must, of course, be understood that this classification of centres of the Brass trade into
Hindu and Muhammadan is not rigidly adhered to, i.e., vessels of the Musalmán type are manufactured in Benares, and vice versá in Moradabad, but in the main the classification holds good.

To commence with Benares :—

Known to all Hindus as Káshi, Benares under this name is frequently mentioned in ancient
writings, though when and why it first acquired a reputation for sanctity and became a noted place
of pilgrimage is a matter altogether uncertain. Equally difficult to trace is its rise as the seat of a
large brass and copper manufacturing centre, and it is an interesting question whether there is not
an intimate connection between its two developments. This point will be discussed in the next
section. Putting aside a comparatively slight manufacture of household utensils, the rest of the
goods produced at Benares are all of an ornamental type—brass idols, brass and copper sacrificial
implements, *phúl* bells, open work brass shields, embossed panels, and brass trays relieved with copper.
Besides there of late years has sprung up a large manufacture of goods of European type—paper
knives," Jardinières," salvers, and other crudities to catch the eye of the guileless *cold weather* bird
of passage. The free communications between the West and East have had a disastrous effect on
Benares work generally : the original native work has to be scamped, left coarse, and unfinished if it
is to keep pace with the rate of demand, while of the new industry of transferring native designs
and pattern to articles of European shape and use, the less said the better ; a Brummagem idol
would hardly be less happy in effect.

Besides the large trade that Benares does with the West, the demand in India for her goods is
very great, each pilgrim that goes to Káshi usually taking away several *Bandrei lotas* and other
mementoes to distribute among his friends at home.

But the mention of *lot*s carries us to Mirzapur, the great centre of manufacture of Hindu
domestic utensils. There the Thatheri Bazár is full of shops, piled high with rows and rows of *lotas,
badnas,* and *thális,* and every day are to be seen bullock carts loaded with these articles on their way
to the neighbouring districts. The railborne traffic is also large, and there are few districts in the
Province to which the Mirzapur *lota* and *thálí* have not found their way.

Lucknow is, or rather *was*, one of the chief centres of manufacture of Muhammadan ornamental
ware. But though the quality of work turned out is still good, the trade is declining. Nor are
the causes far to seek. Ever since the annexation of Oudh, Lucknow city has been growing
poorer, while, on the other hand, the Mutiny ruined the better and wealthier class of Muhammadan
gentry, so that we have at once a contraction of capital at the centre of the manufacture and
diminished demand outside for the goods produced. To balance this failing demand in India for
her goods, Lucknow, unlike Moradabad, has been unable to establish any strong European demand
for her goods, probably because the paper knife and match box do not form any part of her outturn.
The chief articles manufactured at Lucknow are *khdndáns, pindáns, badhnás,* and *sais,* and in plain
household vessels, *deychi* and *patilis.* Some of these *sais* or chased trays are of a very high order
of workmanship.

Moradabad is a town of comparatively modern origin and is chiefly famous for its lacquered
work. Whether this originated in Moradabad or whether it was imported from Kashmir or Persia,
I have been unable to ascertain. The higher class of Moradabad work in which black lacquer is
chiefly used is very beautiful and fully deserves the reputation that it has made. But the gaudy red
and blue vulgarisms that are generally offered for sale, the candlesticks, ash tray, &c., are of no
artistic merit and are one more example of the disastrous effect of European competition on native

handicrafts. The Moradabad workman develops his patterns from his head as he goes on, and consequently the more time he is allowed the better his work. But the rage for cheap prices and the expedition which is necessary in executing European orders has debased his craft, though it may, on the principle of small profits and quick returns, have slightly benefited his pocket. A description of the *modus operandi* of the Moradabad workman will be found in Chapter IV.

Farukhabad, like Mirzapur, is a producer of strictly useful articles—*lota lontiddrs* or *badhus*, *dryekis*, *pilles*, and other domestic utensils of Muhammadan use forming the main outturn of its manufactories. There are 104 factories, chiefly of small size, in the city, affording employment to about 450 hands. Its position for trade is not so favourable as Mirzapur, as it is off the line of railway, but in spite of this the yearly exports to Cawnpore and elsewhere are very large.

Section 9.—Mr. Baines, on page 196 of his Census Report of 1881, remarks :" There is a curious affinity between brass work and Brahmanism" and proceeds to instance, in support of his statement, Benares, Poona, and Nasik—centres at once of Brahmanical influence, and also of a large brass and copper trade. But it is a question, whether on further examination this affinity can really be established. To apply the rule to the North-Western Provinces and Oudh we have as the chief centres of pilgrimage the following :—

Connection between Brahmanish and Brass work.

Benares (Kashi).
Allahabad (Prayag).
Hardwar.
Brindaban.
Ajodhiya.

At none of these, save Benares, is there any brass work of commercial importance carried on. Turning on the other hand, we have as the chief centres of brass trade in Provinces—

Benares.
Mirzapur.
Lucknow.
Moradabad.
Agra.
Farukhabad, and others.

Yet none of these, with the exception of Benares, are places of pilgrimage. Leaving the North-Western Provinces and going further a-field, we have notable resorts of pilgrims, such as Gaya and Puri, destitute of any really valuable brass trade, balanced, on the other hand, by places such as Ajmir and Mysore and Delhi, whose productions in brass and copper have obtained a world-wide reputation while their virtue, if any, as places of pilgrimage remains yet to be discovered.

It is not denied that in many places of pilgrimage, notably Allahabad and Mathura, one peculiar form of the brass trade has sprung up in connection with the shrine whither the pilgrims wend their steps. But such articles as a *Prāyāgi lota* or *Baideo katora* are nothing more than *souvenirs de pélérinage*, and to say that these exert a real influence on the brass trade of the country would be little less exaggeration than to say that Christianity promoted the wood trade by reason of the small olive-wood *souvenirs* that pilgrims to Jerusalem and the Mount of Olives carry back with them on their homeward journey.

Section 10.—In the earlier sections of this chapter the imports and exports of brass and copper, and the wages and profits of those engaged in this industry and the chief centres of the industry, have been dealt with. It now remains to sum up the whole subject, and see whether the brass trade can at present be said to be in a flourishing condition or not.

Present condition of the brass and copper trade.

We must first consider the conditions that predispose to a flourishing state of a trade. They are a strong and effective demand for the products of trade, coupled with a possibility of obtaining at a cheap rate the raw material necessary for the outturn of these products. How far are these conditions realised in the brass trade at present ? As regards the first point, though in many cases the ordinary peasant has merely expended his improved wages on increasing his family, there can be little doubt that the general standard of comfort has risen. This in its turn must entail an increase in the demand for brass and copper vessels in a country where such articles are in a certain sense the measure of a man's social status. Were there any doubt on this point, the increase in the import of brass and copper into the North-Western Provinces and Oudh in the last few years must re-assure us, and this bring us to the question of the price of this new metal. Improved machinery at home for the extraction and preparation of copper ore and brass sheets, combined with the deadly competition between the various lines of steamers trading to the East, have so reduced the cost of importation of raw metal that it can now be landed up-country at an extremely small price. Here then we have the most favourable conditions realized, and yet almost everywhere we are met with the same bitter cry that trade is declining. Confirmed grumbler and *laudator temporis acti* as the Indian manufacturer is known to be, it is inconceivable that such a general complaint should entirely lack foundation. There are, in my opinion, two causes to account for it. The same phenomenon which occurred in England early in this century on the introduction of machinery is reproducing itself in India in a modified form. Under European influence trade is concentrating itself in large cities. The small manufacturer, with his son and possibly one *mazdur* to help him, living perhaps in a town distant many miles from the main railways, has little chance in competition with the large city firm, with its numerous hands and abundant facilities for obtaining the raw supplies for its manufactures. The same report is sent in from all the small manufacturing towns, that their local industries are swamped by the cheap importations from the large centres of manufacture, which railways and improved means of communication have now rendered possible. The only branch of the trade that has in some measure stood its ground is the manufacture of woman's ornament—why, it is hard to say; but the fact remains that isolated Kaseras are still to be met with in remote villages, working at this branch of their trade, though all the cooking pots and pans used in the same village will probably come from the nearest large manufacturing town. Even this survival, it is said, is threatened by the depreciation of silver and consequent rejection of brass and other alloys for a more noble metal.

This is sufficient explanation of the complaint as regards small towns, but what about the large manufacturing towns, where we hear precisely the same cry raised? Here the complaint appears based on a misconception. Owing to the importation of sheet brass and sheet copper, that are easily worked and call for no furnaces or other fusing appliance, the monopoly of the trade is no longer confined to Kaseras and Thatheras and hence, though the aggregate profits of the trade may have considerably increased, the individual profits of some of the older manufacturers possibly have diminished—a state of affairs on which the older manufacturers may be excused if they look with disapprobation.

Lastly, there comes the question, whether English influence has in any way inclined natives to the adoption of china and glass in lieu of the ordinary metal vessels. With the exception of a few Anglicized Hindus and a certain number of richer Muhammadans of the modern school, there are no signs, it may be safely said, yet visible of a general adoption of china and glass ware. As the Anglo-Indian housewife knows to her cost, the ordinary native is not remarkable for careful handling of glass china. Hence in a peasant's house, where the expenditure of every pice is a matter of moment, a fragile plate would scarcely be a desideratum. Hindus as a body are debarred at present from using this kind of ware, owing to their peculiar ideas on the ceremonial purity and impurity. Muhammadans alone are left, and among them only the richer class could afford the luxury of such ware as an article of daily use. There is no danger then of brass and copper vessels being supplanted at any rate at present, by any other kind of ware. In India itself, owing to a higher standard of comfort, the demand for brass and copper vessels is increasing, while the export trade from such places as Benares and Moradabad to England and the west generally, is daily growing larger. True, the smaller towns have suffered loss; this, however, is an inevitable development of commerce, which, much as it may be deplored, it is impossible to prevent; but as regards the main centres of the brass and copper industries in the North-Western Provinces, we are justified in saying that there was never a time when they were more flourishing or prosperous.

CHAPTER III.

Section 1.—The primary metals used in the production of copper and alloy ware are four in number—copper, zinc, tin or pewter, and lead.

Copper, called in Hindustani *támbá*, is one of the metals most anciently known.

It has a reddish-brown colour, inclining to yellow, a faint but nauseous and disagreeable taste, and when rubbed between the fingers imparts a smell somewhat analogous to its taste.

It is much more malleable than it is ductile, so that far finer bars can be obtained from it than wire. Copper in its raw state is imported from Calcutta and Bombay, in blocks, rods, and sheets. The variations in its selling price from district to district are enormous, and it seems impossible to discover any rule to account for the variations. It might be supposed that distance from, or proximity to, the main lines of railway would exert some effect on the range of prices; but this really seems to have very little to do with the matter, in some cases even it contradicts preconceived notions. For instance, in Lucknow, which is a large junction and on the main line of the Oudh and Rohilkhand, we have the price of copper sheets as high as Rs. 49 per maund, while in Sultánpur, which is off the railway, copper sheets sell for Rs. 27-8-0 per maund. Of course some of these divergences may be accounted for by the fact that the quality of the copper is different : but this would only cover variations of from only Rs. 2 to Rs. 5, judging from districts (such as Unao, to which several kinds of copper are imported). The real moral to be drawn from these figures appears to me to be that railways and improved means of transit have not equalized prices all over the country to the extent that is popularly supposed, and that it is still possible for the importers of the raw metal to make a 'corner' to keep up its price. Copper is imported in five different qualities :—

(1) *Záfiráni.*—The best kind of copper and most largely used in making alloys. The name is derived from the Arabic *Zá'afora*, meaning "be dyed with saffron."

(2) *Jajhar.*—The copper remaining from the sheets from which pice have been cut in the Bombay and Calcutta Mints.

(3) *Lodhra.*—Japanese copper (so called perhaps from *lodhra*, a bark used for tanning and dyeing.)

(4) *Jahází.*—Old copper plates, broken from disused vessels (from P. *jahás*, a ship).

(5) *Bhángar.*—Copper shavings and refuse, including old and broken vessels (probably Sans. *Bhanga*=broken).

At one time one extra good kind of copper for making alloys used to be imported into Benares; it was called *Támbá rusiá* (Russian), but it is now no longer imported. It must be added that these five qualities are not imported into every district : one district will import nothing but *Záfaráni*, while another district will import only *Jajhar*. In some districts no difference in the standard of the copper imported is recognised, and the names of the various qualities noted above are absolutely unknown.

Zinc native name, *jasta*—Is a bluish-white metal of considerable lustre and susceptible of polish. In ingots and castings it is brittle, though tough in sheets, and is more tenacious than either tin or lead. It appears to have been originally introduced into Europe from India, whence, as in the similar case of muslin and calico, it has returned in such volume as to oust the original native product. It is now generally imported in the form of small bricks and is sold at prices varying from 10 to 18 rupees per maund, but the general range of prices from district to district is more constant than in the case of copper.

Tin or pewter—native name, Tin and *ránga*.—I have grouped these two together as primary metals, though in reality the latter is an alloy of the former. But although scientifically this is an error, natives generally regard *ránga* as a pure metal and use it as such, that is to say, tin and pewter are used as alternatives. To make bell-metal the same amount either of tin or of pewter will be used. The use of pure tin appears to be very recent; no native name exists for the metal, and it is only in the more go-ahead manufacturing towns that it appears to be ousting pewter.

Tin in general appearance is white, approaching silver, and has a metallic lustre. It is malleable, ductile, and tenacious, and heavier than zinc. Pewter is a tin alloy of most uncertain composition; some state it to be an alloy of 20 parts of tin to one of copper, while others say that it is an alloy of tin and lead. But whatever the other component metal be, whether copper or lead, its volume is always very insignificant in comparison with the tin with which it is mixed.

Lead—native name *sísá*.—This metal is very little used in the manufactures with which this monograph has to deal. It occasionally forms part of one of the inferior kinds of bell-metal.

Section 2.—The question of alloys is not an easy one, owing to the diversity of nomenclature throughout the province. However, after tabulating and comparing the accounts of alloys, contained in the various District Reports, the following appear to be the three principal alloys used in the North-Western Provinces at present :—

Alloy.

English name of alloy.	Native name of alloy.	Copper.	Zinc.	Tin or Pewter.
1. Brass	Pítal	{ 2 / 1·5	1 / 1	
2. Prince's metal ...	Kaskut, Bharat, Kánsá	1	1	
3. Bell-metal ...	Phúl, Kánsá ...	4	...	1

(1) The proportions given for the constituency of the brass alloy vary enormously. The predominating mixtures are, however, 1·5 of copper to 1 of zinc and 2 of copper to 1 of zinc. The former corresponds to the proportions given in Ure* for Muntz's metal, and the latter is what is known in England as good yellow brass. As a matter of fact in this country alloys in general and the brass alloy in particular are mixed chiefly by rule of thumb, or tradition handed down from father to son, and there is no attempt at the scientific accuracy and preciseness with which English alloys are made. Added to this, as Pandit Janardan Joshi remarks in his Bareilly Report, the manufacturers are very chary of letting strangers into the secrets of their trade, each Thathera imagining that his method of alloying is superior to that of his neighbours. Consequently it is possible that some of the abnormal alloys that are reported from one or two districts may really be due to intentional misinformation on the part of the manufacturers.

Though brass is one of the alloys most widely used in the manufacture of native vessels, whether of domestic use or of ornament, but little is actually made in India. The great majority is imported in the form of sheets from England, this being found more economical and satisfactory in every way. The price of brass at current rates is given below.

(2) *Kaskut, Bharat, or Kánsá.*—This alloy varies but little in composition, though much in name all over the province, and appears from its proportions to correspond with what is known as Prince's metal in England.* It is variously known as *Kaskut, Bharat, or Kánsá*, though this latter name is in some districts, such as Aligarh, applied to bell-metal. It is almost invariably used for casting purposes, and being by far the cheapest of the three alloys, is in great demand as a material for the *batués* and other cooking pots of the poorer classes and for cheap ornament for women. The colour of *Kaskut* is somewhere between that of brass and bell-metal, but it has not the sheen of the latter composition.

Phúl or Kánsá.—This is the most constant of the three alloys and answers both in its use and its proportions to the bell-metal of English commerce. It is also sometimes termed white brass on account of its colour, being much lighter in hue than ordinary brass. Owing to the high finish which it will take, *phúl* is very largely used in the manufacture of ornaments, *huqqa* stands, and other similar articles ; domestic utensils made of it are much prized, as owing to the presence of tin in its composition, acids do not affect this alloy. Its cost, however, considerably diminishes the demand for it for the latter purpose.

The following are the prices at which the three abovementioned alloys sell :—

Name of alloy.				Price per ser.
Brass				14 annas to 1 rupee.
Kaskut				10 annas to 14 annas.
Phúl				1 Re. to Re. 1-8-0, or even more.

* URE.—Dictionary of Arts and Manufactures, Vol. 1, page 101.

Section 3.—There is hardly any limit to the number of times old metal can be worked up into new vessels, and in some districts the collection of old metal for export to the chief centres of the brass manufacture forms quite a trade by itself. Old and broken vessels in this country are never thrown away, as is the case so often in England, but are either sold to the itinerant dealers, who perambulate the country collecting old metal, or in districts where there are large manufactures of brass ware, as in Mirzapur, the purchaser of a new vessel gives the old vessel as part price of his new purchase. Old metal is generally worked up into trays and similar vessels by the process described below in sections 15 to 17. In Gorakhpur the indigo factories buy up large quantities for making the nuts, &c., of the indigo presses. In fact, as in the case of its relation, 'the old kerosine oil'tin,' there seems no limit to the uses to which old brass and copper vessels can be put. The general price for all old metal is said to be at Rs. 20 per maund, though in some districts old copper and páil range somewhat higher, e. g., in Sháhjáhánpur the price of old brass is Rs. 21-4-0 per maund, and old copper Rs. 29 per maund. In Gorakhpur, old brass is quoted at annas 8 per ser, old copper at annas 0-8-1 per ser, and old páil at annas 0-8-4 per ser. In bartering old vessels against new, the old vessel is valued at from ¼ to ⅖ its original price.

Old metal.

Section 4.—A flux is any ingredient which is mixed with metals or alloys, to aid their fusion or to clarify them when fused. The most common fluxes used in India are ordinary salt, *namak*, borax (*sohágá*), and *sajji*, a kind of refuse salt. Besides fluxes there are a certain number of *masolas* or chemical mixtures and preparations used with the intention of perfecting the colour of the alloy. The most common of these is sal ammoniac (*nausádar*), but in special cases powdered corrosive sublimate (*raskapur*) and bones are used. If the alloy is still discoloured, a little powdered dogs' dung is found to have a good effect. The following process is reported to be in use in Aligarh for improving the colour of alloys :—

Fluxes, colouring matter, and solders used.
(a) Fluxes.

A flat plate of alloy weighing about 4 chhaták is laid on cow dung fuel cakes with the following powder scattered both above and below it :—

					Chhaták.
Salt ...	...	...	...	...	1
Nausádar	...	...	...	...	1
Alum ...	...	...	...	...	1
Red earth (*geru*)	...	...	...	...	2
Old red *pakka* bricks	...	...	...	4

The fuel cakes are then set fire to, and when they are completely burnt, the plates are taken out and cleaned with some acid.

Solder is generally known as *Ránj* in Hindustáni, though at Benares we find the Persian word *Mirjosh* (*mis* copper ; *joshidán*, to boil) in common use. The constituent parts vary according to the metal it is proposed to join, e. g., in Benares the solder for copper vessels is composed of four chhaták of copper to five of pewter, that for brass vessels of 4 chhaták copper to one of pewter, that for páil vessels of 7 tolas of páil to one tola pewter. In Lucknow the ingredients differ somewhat, pewter being replaced by zinc and borax being added. In Sháhjáhánpur a curious solder composed of zinc and bell-metal and called *kasaura* is employed. In many of the less important manufacturing districts a solder of copper and zinc of uniform consistence is used for all vessels, whether composed of copper, brass, or any other alloy. The solder is generally ground to a powder and mixed into a wet paste. In this form it is lightly spread over the dove-tailed joint of the two parts of the vessel that are to be united, and then fused and hammered in.

(b) Solders.

PART I.

Section 5.—The casting process is the most widely extended of the two methods of manufacture in this Province. In many districts the art of beating out brass and copper vessels is unknown, but there are very few towns of note that do not boast of some kind or other of manufacture by casting. The casting process naturally falls into two sub-divisions—moulding and casting proper.

The casting process.

Section 6.—The ordinary clays used for moulding are *kāli* or *chiknī mitti*, a heavy dark clay generally found by tanks and similar places, called also *kumhāroti*, *kamoṭhi*, and *jaṭao*; *pili mitti*, a lighter, yellowish coloured clay; *balua mitti*, a yellow, sandy earth: this is replaced in some districts, by what is known as *bimaut* or ant-hill soil. Various ingredients are used to strengthen these clays; for this purpose the moulder adds rice husks, bájrá husks, chopped *munj* and *bán*, cotton, horse dung, cow dung, and blinea. These clays, with the strengthening additions I have just noted, form the ordinary material from which moulds are made; but in some districts special preparations are used. In Aligarh the moulds in which padlocks are cast, are made from a mixture of clay, rosin, and oil, and those destined for the manufacture of ornaments are generally formed of a composition of sand, beroza, and castor oil. Oil appears to be very commonly used in preparing the clay in which small or fine castings are to be made, its effect being to render the clay more plastic in the hands of the moulder.

The clays used.

Section 7.—To a casual observer this might seem a somewhat simple process, but this is not really the case. The mould (*sānchā*) is evolved through a number of stages, which have each their own recognised name and importance. The names of these different intermediate stages differ from district to district, as do also the number and character of the stages. Generally speaking, the larger the manufactories, the greater is the care bestowed on the moulding and the more numerous the stages by which the mould is built up. Each mould, however, consists of two portions—the inner core, which is generally known as *gabhā*, and the other shell, *palla*. We will now proceed to describe the making of mould, after the Benares or Mirzapur fashion.

The moulding process.

(1) The moulder (*sānchā*) forms a small shallow cup or saucer either upon a block shape or by rule of thumb. This is termed *dhibrī*.

(2) Next, he forms the upper piece, which is termed *spalli* and may roughly be described as funnel shaped.

(3) The third step is to join the *dhibrī* and *spalli*, the funnel being inverted.

(4) A lump of clay, fashioned into the form of a cap and expressively called *ṭopaki*, is fixed on the top of the *spalli*, forming a thick brim that extends about an inch beyond the *spalli*. This cap is termed *ár* or *ṭikiyā* in Unao.

Note.—These four processes are known collectively in Benares as *gabhā*.

(5) The embryo mould is now coated with a mixture of cow dung and *balua mitti*, which has the effect of strengthening and cementing the various parts together. This step is called *gubrāhā*.

(6) Additional coats of clay and sandy earth are plastered on to raise the mould to the requisite size. This step is konwn as *mitāhā*.

(7) All that is now required is to finish off the inner core. This is done by means of a rough lathe termed *saryá*.

This *sargá*, called at Benares *salagá* and elsewhere *salgá*, consists of a rod of iron 14 to 15 inches long and pointed at both ends. One end of the *sargá* is fixed loosely in a notch in an upright peg, *khunta*; the other end is fixed in a ball of mud and rests against a round mallet head, *mungari*, which is laid horizontally on the ground and kept in its place by a stone flag as a dead weight. In Benares the *sargá* is not fixed in a ball of mud, but in a hole in the *mungari*. The mould is transfixed by the *sargá*, and is replaced between its two supports at an angle of about 30,° so that the broader part of the mould, which is nearer the *khunta* may not touch the earth as it revolves. Sometimes the *sargá* is fixed horizontally and the earth between the two supports hollowed out, to effect the same purpose. A *ghará* of water is generally sunk flush with the ground, close at hand, into which a rag is occasionally dipped and passed over the surface of the mould as it revolves. The lathe being fixed, the operator sits before it, with his scraper *khardaal* or *koj-ni*, a small strip of iron, in his right hand; with his left hand he keeps the mould a-spinning and with his right hand resting on the *phirui*, a square of wood, supported by a handle in the middle, he deftly plies the *khardani*, peeling off the superfluous clay and in a short time turns out a perfectly finished core.

(8) We now leave the inner core and proceed to the manufacture of the outer shell.

Fresh clay is plastered either on to the core that has just been made, if dry enough, or on to some old core of a similar size. This is smoothed down, and when dry or nearly so, cut in half, the result giving two kinds of caps, called *pallá*.

(9) These *pallá* are then applied to the core, which they fit more or less exactly, and are plastered over with cow dung and more clay. This step is termed *lakes* in Benares.

(10) When dry the *pallás* are again opened and removed from the *gabái*.

(11) The *gabái* is then again put on the lathe and enough clay scraped away all round to give room for the requisite thickness of metal which it is desired to give to the vessel. To preserve this thickness and to keep the outer shell equidistant all round from the core, small brass nails are fixed down into the inner core and left projecting the required distance. The same purpose is effected in other districts by a layer of wax between the inner and outer moulds; occasionally in the case of large castings where much support is necessary to the outer shell, both nails and wax are used. The use of wax is the ordinary European method.

(12) The *pallás* are then again put on to the inner core and joined up with a coating of clay and *balui mitti*, the operator fixing them firmly at the top of the mould to the inner core. This prevents any shifting of the relative positions of the core and outer mould which would destroy the evenness of the cast. The step is called *jor*.

(13) The mould is now flattened at the top, inverted, and a small funnel-shaped hole left at the bottom, through which the molten metal is eventually poured.

Lastly, a fresh coating of the strongest clay, mixed with paddy husks and cow dung, is plastered all over the mould, to give it strength to stand the baking and other rough usage to which it is subjected before receiving the molten metal.

The method of moulding just described is rather complicated: simpler methods exist, as for instance in Meerut. There the outer shell is first made, on an old vessel, and when dry is cut in two, taken off the old vessel and joined up again. The inside of the mould is dusted with ashes inside and then plastered with strong clay, which plaster, by reason of the ashes, does not adhere to the outer mould. The outer mould is then again opened and the inner lathed and scraped; nails or wax are then inserted to keep the two moulds at a proper distance apart; the outer shell is replaced and plastered over with a strong coating of clay and the mould is ready to be baked.

Both the methods, whether of the Benares or Meerut kind, described above only apply to the moulding of vessels of the shape of *batuds*, *lotás*, &c., which are hollow inside. Mouldings for solid castings are a much simpler matter. I quote the following extract from the Report of the Etáwah district, compiled by the then Assistant Magistrate, Mr. H. R. C. Dobbs:—

"The whole method will easily be understood from an example. I will take the manufacture of a *karra* or anklet. The workman (in this case a *kasbhara* or worker in bell-metal) takes a strip of clay, rolls it into his hands into a round shape, and joins it into a ring. He then presses an old *karra* into the ring thus formed and removes it, leaving the reverse impression of one side of the *karra*. This strip of clay is called a *pallá*. A second *pallá* is then made, fine wood ashes are scattered over the impression left on each *pallá*, and the two are clapped together. The crack, *daoj*, between them is plastered over with common clay, a hole called *muárá* being left for the entrance of the molten metal above the serpent's head. Five or six of these moulds are then stuck together side by side, the *muárds* at the top of each forming a straight line. A funnel of clay is then built up round the openings."

In Lucknow, Agra, and Benares permanent moulds of stone and iron are used, chiefly for solid castings. The moulds of this kind in use at Lucknow consist of two horse-shoe shaped frames of iron, which can be clamped together. The nether frame is placed on a board and filled with ordinary earth, which is rammed down and made quite even; an impression of the article to be cast is then made on the earth, to about half the thickness of the article. The upper frame is similarly treated, a small channel for the molten metal is left, and the two frames are clamped together. The mould is then ready for the reception of the molten metal. This process is so remarkably like the methods in vogue in England and other European countries that in all probability it has been only recently introduced into India. We do not see these permanent moulds used anywhere except in large manufacturing towns.

The methods described in this section practically represent all the processes used for moulding at the present time in this province, with the exception of one or two processes peculiar to ornamental work, which will be described in their proper place in Chapter IV.

Section 8.—The crucible and main tools used in the *casting process :*—

The crucible, known generally as the *ghariya*, is built of the same kind of clay as the mould, and the same strengthening materials, *viz.*, paddy husks, cow dung, &c., are worked into the composition. In some districts chalk is also added, probably because it stands the action of fire very well. The crucible is built on a standard crucible, inverted : its size varies much, depending, of course, on the quality intended to be fused in it : some will be built to contain only one ser of metal, some large enough to hold twenty sers. The shape of the crucible varies somewhat according as to whether it is to be joined to the mould or left separate, for in many districts, when only small castings are made, the crucible is solidly joined to the mould, both are put into the furnace at the same time, and when fusion has taken place, the joint mould and crucible are merely inverted, so that the molten metal may run into the mould below. If the crucible be destined for this method of casting, it is made U-shaped and its mouth is left open till it is joined to the mould. If, however, it is intended, as is generally the case in large castings, that the crucible shall remain separate from the mould, it is built somewhat after the shape of a ewer, the top closed in, and a small hole left in one side, near the top. This hole contrives a double debt to pay : from it the founder pours the molten metal into the mould, and by watching it during the process of fusion he is able to tell by the coloured vapour that issues from it whether or no the metal is ready for running.

In the majority of districts crucibles are made in mode No. 2. In Benares both kinds are used—the joint crucible for small castings, the separate crucible for large ones.

Another common name for the crucible is *bolá*, a word of Persian origin. Rarer still is the word *kuthálí*, which appears to be of local usage in the two adjoining districts of Sahâranpur and Muzaffarnagar and is evidently of Panjáb use.[a] (It is derived from the Sans. Kuṭhárika.)

Before commencing the description of the actual casting process it may be as well to summarize briefly the chief tools used for this process :—

Sásd.—First and most important of all the tools used in casting is the *sansd*, a large pair of tweezers, with one or more bends used for taking crucibles out of the fire. The name is also spelt *sáṛhsá* and *sáṇdásá.*

Kalchhi.—A kind of ladle or iron skimmer, used for picking up the molten metal which drops on the floor, in pouring from the crucible into the moulds.

Baskli.—Used to remove the molten metal which accumulates round the hole of the moulds into which the metal is run from the crucible.

Sabrí.—A pointed instrument, used to make the hole in the crucible, through which the metal is poured ; also called *soáná* in Benares.

Konch.—Used to take moulds out of the furnace.

Sánsi.—Small tweezers, used for picking up any hot substance.

Section 9.—In most districts where the manufacture of the cast vessels attains to any degree of importance two kinds of furnaces are used—one for making the moulds, and one for fusing the metal in the crucible. These two, though generically known as *bhaṭṭi*, have distinct names in many districts. The mould furnace is known as *koṭhú* in Shâhjahánpur, Sitapur, and Etah : the crucible furnace is called *masturi* in Shâhjahánpur, *masurhi* in Mirzapur, *masturi* in Fatehpur, *morihi* in Partábgarh, *kotka* in Gorakhpur and Bijnor, *dabka* in Bahraich and Gonda, and *dhamsa* in Unao (perhaps from Sans. dham=glow, cf. dhamakná.

The mould furnace (*sanche ki bhaṭṭi*) is built either round or square and is from five to six feet high by three to four feet in diameter. It is made of bricks, thickly coated with mud. A little more than halfway down is fixed a rough lattice framework of clay, generally made of bits of old crucibles ; on this the moulds are placed to bake. Beneath this again lies the fuel which is introduced

The furnace.

---

[a] Panjáb Monograph for 1886-87, paragraph 11.

by a small aperture in the side of the *bhatti* below the frame. In some districts the top of the furnace is covered with a roughly shaped dome, in others slabs of indurated clay are slid over the top of the *bhatti* to prevent the heat escaping.

The crucible furnace or *mál kí bhatti* is generally sunk three feet below the surface of the ground and projects to about two feet above. It is almost invariably circular in shape and has ordinarily a diameter of from four to six feet. The same latticed platform is constructed halfway down the cylinder on which to rest the crucibles. An aperture is made below the platform, by which to feed the furnace, and near this are let in two ducts (*dhudiá*). These connect with the nozzle of the bellows (*khál, kháli, or dhaunkwi*) and thus introduce the blast into the lower chamber of the furnace; thence it escapes through the lattice platform and finally makes its exit through the slits left for this purpose between the slabs that cover the top of the furnace. The fuel used is usually cow dung, charcoal, and wood. A layer of fuel cakes is first spread and covered loosely with charcoal and wood.

Section 10.—Having now described the moulds, tools, crucibles, and furnaces used in casting, we are in position to go on to the actual process of casting. The moulds and crucibles being arranged in their appropriate furnaces, lighted coals are introduced through the furnace door; a bright fire is maintained in either furnace for some five hours, the temperature in the crucible furnace being artificially raised by the forced blast from the bellows. The heat in the casting room is intense: in many places, in order to mitigate this evil, the furnaces only work at night, but in Mirzapur I have found them in full blast on a steamy July afternoon. In spite of the heat, the casting room is rather a picturesque sight, with its semi-darkness relieved now and then by a fitful lurid glare from the furnace, as the dusky workmen shove the slabs aside and shake the crucible, to test the state of the molten metal. As soon as the vapour issuing from the hole in the crucible (section 8) shows by its peculiar colour that the metal is properly fused, the moulds are removed from their furnaces and ranged along the floor of the casting shed in a row.

The *dhálía* or caster then switches out a crucible from the *bhatti* with a pair of long tweezers (*sánsi*) and commences pouring in the molten metal through the small aperture (*munhra*) left in the mould. As he does this another operative gently taps the mould, to insure a perfect permeation of the fluid metal. In factories where the joint mould and crucible are used, the workmen test the state of the metal by shaking the crucible, and when they judge it to have reached the proper stage, reverse the position of mould and crucible so that the fluid metal pours of itself into the mould beneath. The pouring in of the fused metal into the crucible is termed *dhárái, dhalái, or dharkái*, derived from the verb *dhálná or dhárna* meaning " to pour ". When the molten metal has been run into the moulds, they are allowed to stand some five to six hours to cool. Any undue haste in breaking up the mould before the metal had set would mean spoiling the casting.

Section 11.—When the mould is broken in the morning and the vessel emerges, it is of a greeny colour and in a very rough condition, even when not actually defective. It is then passed on the *rítía* or filer (so called because he uses the file (*reti*)), who files off the inequalities of the surface and beats it where necessary into shape. The tools which the *rítía* uses are the following :—

(1) The wooden *kharwaí*, a two pronged triangular piece of wood, in the apex of which the vessel is fixed when under the file.

(2) The iron *kharwaí*, a heavy piece of rod iron, turned up at one end to give it a firm hold when pressed against the wall and flattened at the other. This flattened end is introduced into the vessel, and acts as a kind of anvil, on which the filer can remedy any minor defects of shape by beating with the hammer.

(3) *Chháni*, or iron chisel, used for striking off the nails from the vessel.

(4) The *reti*, or file, of two kinds, round and flat.

When the *rítía* has accomplished his task, he passes the vessel on to the *kuuwa or khardái*, or lathe man, for him to polish. The lathe deserves some description. Its nomenclature varies a good deal from district to district; in districts in the centre and to the east of the province it is generally known as *kúnd, kúnj, kúng, or kún*; while in Oudh and the northern districts it is called *khardá* or *charakî*. In one dis'rict, Unao, it is known as *châk*, the ordinary word in Hindi for a potter's wheel. Various as are its appellations its form remains constant. The lathe itself is made of *babîl* or catechu wood and consists of a heavy roller, thicker at one end and tapering somewhat at the other, usually about 4½ feet from end to end. The thick end of this roller is fixed into a peg (*khuntâ*) driven into the ground. About six inches from the other end, the roller rests loosely in a piece of wood, called the *ndk* or nose, projecting from a heavy block of wood, termed the *baghcli*. On the outward side of the *baghcli* and directly underneath the tapering end of the roller is dug a hollow in the ground, into which the scrapings of the metal fall. Round that part of the roller which lies between the peg and the *baghcli* is wound a strap *dirôli* (properly *dûdli*, from Persian *dûdî* leather), *tasma*, *baddhi* generally made of leather and from 14 to 15 feet long. The *kâinchwd* then heats the vessel that is to be lathed and affixes it by means of scaling wax (lâh-lac) to the thin end of the roller. When the joint has grown cold and firm, he squats on one side of the *kund* and commences pulling the strap backwards and forwards. As soon as the vessel commences to revolve, the *kunwâ* applies his various chisels and turning instruments. These are known generally as *lahni* and *randi*; the number and shape of them vary much from district to district, as also their names, so that to give a lengthy catalogue of them would be of little use or profit. The *kunwd* rests his hand on a wooden *phorwi*, described above in section 7. Under his skilful handling, the rough, coarse casting of the early morning soon assumes a fine sheeny appearance, the turning on the lathe giving it a very high finish. This, especially in the case of brass goods, is still further enhanced by polishing the vessel with *tezdb* or nitric acid. Other less potent acids are used for this purpose, mention of which will be made in section 17 of this chapter.

Section 12.—It is a by no means uncommon occurrence to find, when the mould is broken up, that the casting is defective. For instance, the metal may not have properly permeated the mould, or holes may be caused by the air not having been able to escape properly as the metal was run in. Flaws are also caused by too rapid cooling. It has been calculated that nearly 25 per cent. of the castings are usually found defective.

Defective castings.

Section 13.—Should the flaw be very great, there is nothing for it but to melt down the vessel and recast it. But in some districts, when the flaw is slight, they have an ingenious method of repairing the defective vessel. This is done by laying on a patch, called *chakti* or *thik*, cut from a new sheet of the same metal. The process of mending will vary according as the vessel is one of pure brass or of alloy. In the former case four teeth *dântâ* are made in the patch, to grip the edge of the hole in the vessel, and the patch is then beaten on with a mallet, *hathowrâ*. In the latter case the edges of the patch and of the hole in the vessel are filed until they are even and fit properly, when they are soldered together with *rânj*. *Rânj* is a solder composed of brass and copper, ground into powder and made into a paste. In the case of small holes, it is sufficient merely to fill them in with *rânj*, without laying on any patch.

How repaired.

PART II.

Section 14.—This falls naturally into two heads—beating from native cast plates and beating from English sheet brass. It is interesting to note how far the latter process is ousting the former. From the reports that have been submitted, it is evident that the English sheet metal is used at the chief centres of the trade, to the entire or almost entire exclusion of the native cast plate. Thus at Lucknow, Cawnpore, and Benares nothing but English sheet metal is employed. In Meerut, Farukhabad, Agra, Aligarh, and Mirzapur both systems are in vogue: the native caste plate process is, however, more employed for working up old metal, and though in Agra and Farukhabad new vessels are made in this way, the English sheet metal is said to be displacing the older native metal in these cities also.

The beating process.

The only district of real importance, from the view of this report, that still employs the older system to the entire exclusion of the new is Mainpuri. This is rather hard to understand, but may be accounted for by the fact that it is not on the line of rail. Glancing at the less important centres of manufacture, the processes are found to be fairly evenly divided, with a slight majority on the side of English sheet metal. The choice seems a good deal a matter of chance, since we find that at Unao, which is just between Cawnpore and Lucknow, nothing but native cast plates are used. However this may be, there can be little doubt that in a few years English sheet brass and copper will have completely ousted the older native cast plates, except where the latter process is employed to utilize old metal. And indeed it can only be due to the traditional conservatism of the East that it has not done so already, when one considers the enormous saving of labour, time, and materials effected by the new process. The economic effect of this change has been discussed in an earlier section (vide section 11, Chapter II).

Section 15.—Though every metal and alloy that this report deals with can be treated by this process, still a decided preference is shown to brass, *phúl*,
Native cast plates. and old refuse metal. Any process in which copper alone has to be melted is generally avoided by natives, owing to the high temperature necessary to fuse it; hence the copper trays to be met with in the bazars are generally made from English sheet copper. *Kashut* does not for some reason appear to be a favourite metal for beating vessels. The process that we will now describe applies chiefly to brass and refuse metal as *phúl* is very frequently beaten straight from the lump and not first cast into a plate. In some districts where new vessels are beaten from English sheet brass, the term *gharai* is applied to the beating out of native plates cast from old metal.

The brass founder takes a crucible of the ordinary size and fills it either with old metal or with copper and zinc according to the proportion in use in his district. When the metal is fused it is run into a small round earthen dish.

These are generally about ¾ to ⅛ an inch deep, and vary in diameter from 6 inches to a foot, according to the size of the vessel it is proposed to make: 6 inches is, however, the normal diameter. They are generally known as *paggd* or *pdgd*. When the metal has cooled, the earthen saucer is broken up and the metal plate taken out. This is known in Mirzapur as the *khuti*, in Unao as the *gurí*, in Bijnor and other districts as the *galli*. The latter is the common word in use in the Panjáb.

Section 16.—The next process is to beat out these plates. For this they are first heated in a furnace termed *bhattí pitdí* (*viz.*, the beating furnace), in
How beaten out. which no forced draught is used. When they are red hot, they are taken out from the furnace and beaten out in lots of two, four, six, or even more. The number that can be simultaneously beaten out depends on the size and thickness of the vessels: generally each plate is beaten once separately, before the simultaneous beating commences. The plates are then replaced in the furnace. When red hot one heap is withdrawn with a pair of tweezers, called *kúnch*, and placed on an anvil. In Mirzapur this anvil is made of stone and termed *Gárd*. In some districts it consists of a block of wood (*kútá*), in which is fixed a slab of iron (*nihdí*). In other districts the anvil is of the ordinary sort, made of iron and termed, as usual, *nihdí*. It is sunk in the ground just opposite the furnace mouth. One workman called the *bhániya* holds the heap of *khúti* in place and keeps turning them round on the anvil, while the other workmen called the Pitangá or ghanwá lay on with their heavy hammers (*ghan*, Bijnor-*bdí*).

The workmen display considerable dexterity in wielding these hammers. Each hammer descends in rotation; the leader strikes two blows and then the second man chimes in, and so on, reminding the spectator irresistibly of bell-ringers at home. As soon as one set of *khúti* begins to get cold, it is replaced in the furnace and a second set is withdrawn, the long rod or tweezers (*kúnch*) being used for this purpose. The men rest a short time between each set, as the work is extremely exhausting. In this way it is calculated that from 1 to 2½ maunds of metal can be beaten out in a day. The resulting plates, called *pán* or *pand*, are about $\frac{1}{10}$ of an inch thick and 1½ feet in diameter, though this latter point depends of course on the diameter of the original *khúti*.

Besides the abovementioned process there is a simpler method in vogue in many places for beating out *phúl* or old metal to the requisite thinness necessary for making *thálís*, &c. A lump of *phúl* or old brass is heated over an open furnace, *anna*, and beaten out into a single plate. The *anna* is like a miniature forge and is worked by bellows.

Section 17.—When the plates have reached the *pound* stage already mentioned they are withdrawn from the furnace and allowed to cool. A circle is

Manufacture of vessels for these plates. then drawn on them, roughly corresponding with the size of the vessel that is to be made; the circle is either scratched on the plate with a pointed compass (*parkár, parkál, chundkái*), or marked out with chalk. The plates are then replaced in the furnace and when red-hot, the circle drawn on them is cut out with a pair of clippers (Unao-*kál*; Etáwah-*katarná*). A workman, called the *Mangaryiá*, then takes the plates and holding them in a slanting position on an iron slab, which has a groove (*katarná*) in it, hammers them with a *mangarí* (mallet) round the edge till a side is raised. The plates are then passed on to another workman, to undergo a further hammering, and have their edges filed. The pickling and cleaning process next commences, which occupies some six days. The embryo vessel is placed in an earthen vat (*nánd*) filled with water, in which the dried skins and stones of the mango fruit have been steeped; there it remains until the metal becomes of a yellowish tinge. It is then taken out, rubbed with sand, and polished with tamarind (*imlí*) leaves. Finally, it is scraped clean with a chisel (*lakní*): a most painful process to assist at, since the noise of the *lakní* working is something worse than that of a slate pencil drawn over a slate. The *thálí* is at this stage nothing more than a flat plate, with curved sides; sometimes nothing more is done to it than this, but generally it is passed on to go through a further process of hammering on various anvils, which have each their own name and property. In making *thálís*, however, the number of anvils used is small, but in the production of more ornamental vessels where sharp heads and flowing curves are necessary, as many as six may be employed. The first anvil on which the *thálí* is placed is a short blunt headed iron anvil. The operative holds the *thálí* against the anvil and adds a new feature to it by beating out a sloping side, so that in its final state the ordinary *thálí* is divided into three portions, the bottom, *pendí*, the sloping side, *dhótá*, and the vertical edge, *bagú*. In Mirzapur the *thálí* is then transferred into a sharp pointed anvil, *sabrá*. The workman inverts the *thálí* and holding it so that its centre coincides with the point of the anvil, strikes it a sharp blow with his hammer. After each blow he shifts the tray on about an ⅛th of an inch in an outward circular direction, leaving behind a round bright mark. When he has finished the bottom of the tray, he traces the same simple pattern on the vertical rim (*baglá*), leaving the sloping side plain. The contrast between the bright and dull surfaces has a pleasing effect, and gives an appearance of finish to even the commonest tray. In many districts after the tray has been beaten into shape on the anvil, it is finished by polishing with a chisel (*lakani*) on the lathe, described in section 11 of this chapter.

Section 18.—The methods of beating from English sheet brass and copper is very simple. A circle is drawn on the sheet, the size of the vessel or part of the vessel, which it is intended to make. This is done with a part of compasses, *parkár, parkál*, and the disc is cut out by means of a small stout chisel, *cheni or chaini*, and a hammer, *hora*, or with a pair of rough scissors, *gainchi*. If the sheet be too thick it is beaten to the requisite thinness, and is then passed on to the operatives at the anvils, to beat into the required shape, as described in section 17.

The beating process, however, whether conducted according to the old or new method, produces vessels of such diverse kind and shape from the plain *thálí* that may be picked up in any bazár for a rupee or less, to the costly and elaborate *pándán* and *badhná* of Lucknow pattern, that to attempt to give a detailed account of the methods by which each different class of vessel is produced, would be well nigh impossible and, if accomplished, would swell this monograph to a size far beyond its proper limits. In every case the tools used (*vide* section 19) are much the same all over the province: the results produced differ according to the taste and skill of the individual workman at the various centres of manufacture. A short account of the more notable ornamental processes which are carried out by beating will be found in Chapter IV.

List of tools used in the beating process. **Section 19.**—The anvils used are of the following kind:—

Nikái.—A low square block of iron, fixed into the ground, as is the case with all the other sorts of iron anvils, by a spike. This *nikái* is used for beating metal flat.

Nikái gadhádár.—Differs only from the above in having a depression in the middle. It is used for shaping sheet brass into a curve, the hammer being so directed that it forces the brass into the depression at every stroke of the *hdrí* or *okhlí*.

Gegrá.—A flat block of stone, used for the same purpose as the *siádi.*

Hári or okhli.—A block of stone, with a deep circular dip cut in it. It is used for beating sheet metal into a concave shape and is similar in purpose to the *siádi gadheddr,* but is employed for coarser work.

Sabrá.—A vertical iron rod, with a curved beak-shaped head and square base, surmounting the spike by which it is fixed into the ground. It is used for making sharp bends and indentations.

Sabri or sabra gulmusha.—A thick bar of iron, shaped like a cone and polished. It is used for making the ornamental hammer marks with which *thálís,* &c., are ornamented (*vide* section 17).

Shándán.—T-shaped anvil, used for turning down edges and forming the lips of vessels.

Sandán or itwái.—Somewhat similar to the above, has a sharp cone-shaped spike on one side of its head, and a flat projection, ending in a sharpe rim, on the other. It is used for making line patterns and indentations.

Sáráng.—A slender rod of iron, used for shaping thin strips of brass into rims of vessels and into cylinders. The *saráng* is supported by what is known as a *karod.* This consists of a V-shaped wooden fork attached to a square base, perforated in the middle. Through this hole the *saráng* is passed obliquely, the workman holding one end of it with his toe, while the other end is supported by the *karod.*

The following are the principal hammers used :—

Mungari.—A large hammer of the ordinary native type.

Hathaura.	Ditto ditto	only smaller.

Mathon.—This is bulging at the base and square at the striking part, and is made in three sizes.

Bál.—Is a hammer, with a narrow oblong head. In some districts the same as *Ghan, q. v.*

Báli.—The head of this hammer is sharply pointed on both sides.

Gulmanhá.—A round-headed hammer.

Ghan.—A very heavy, square-headed sledge-hammer. Sometimes called *Bál.*

Miscellaneous tools.

Katarná or káí.—Large clippers, used to cut out discs from native beaten plates when red hot (section 17).

Qainchi.—Small clippers or scissors used for cutting out strips from English sheet metal.

Chhaini or Chheni.—A small wedge-shaped chisel, with no handle, used for the same purpose as the *Qainchi.*

Parkál, Parkár, or Chundkhá.—Compasses for describing circles on sheet metal.

Lahni.—The generic term for a chisel used both for polishing vessels on the lathe, and also for chasing decorative patterns.

Khad, Khará, or Charkh.—The lathe, *vide* section 11, Chapter III.

Sánsi.—Tweezers.

Section 20.—Many of the vessels in daily use are made by a combination of the casting and beating processes, *i.e.,* one part of the vessel is beaten and another cast and then the two parts are soldered together to form the whole. All that has been said above in section 18 as to the diversity in manufacture of beaten vessels applies equally to that of composite vessels, but this report would hardly be complete if it did not convey some idea of how it is possible to combine the two main processes that have been already described. The *gagrá* and *badháú* will be taken as typical examples. To commence with the *gagrá.*

Method of manufacting composite vessels.

On a sheet of copper two circles are described with the compass and cut out by means of the chisel, as has been already described in section 18. The two discs are then placed over the *Hárí* or Okhlí. Into this dip the discs are beaten with a heavy wooden mallet. Under this hammering they gradually assume the shape of a basin and thus form the upper and lower halves of the *gagra*. They are called *mokla* and *prndí* respectively. A hole is then cut in the upper half, for the insertion of the mouthpiece (*mohtár*, *mudhandí*). This mouthpiece is made separately from a cast copper plate (*khurí*, section 15). It is beaten from the centre outwards, with a chisel (*chhení*) and hammer (*sungari*). From time to time, in the course of the beating, the workman beats it over an open furnace (*anna*), to render the copper more malleab'e. When completed it is soldered into the hole made for it in the upper half of the *gagra*. All that now remains to be done is to join the upper and lower halves. The edges are dove-tailed and beaten together and soldered with *ránj* [section 4(*b*)]. This makes a a very strong fastening and enables the *gagra* to stand the rough usage to which it is often subjected. Lastly, the *gagra* is fixed on the lathe and polished up in the manner already described in section 11 of this chapter.

Similarly, in making a *badhna*, the various portions, body, and spout are first hammered out, the rings for the bottom and top are cast, and then the whole joined together with solder *ránj*.

CHAPTER IV.

ORNAMENTAL PROCESSES.

Section 1.—This chapter contains by no means an exhaustive description of all the ornamental

Aim of this chapter.

work of which these provinces can boast. Such a description would be quite beyond the compass of the present report. I have merely attempted in the following sections to indicate what are the chief kinds of ornamental processes in copper and brass work and in what towns they chiefly flourish. The subject of female ornaments has, however, been grouped under one section, as both the products themselves and the methods of producing them are remarkably similar all over the province. By this arrangement it has been possible to save a good deal of unnecessary repetition.

Section 2.—The idol-maker first prepares a mixture of wax and resin termed *moin* and out of

Benares work. (a) Idol casting.

this model's the figure with his hand. The nails of the hand are very dexterously used for marking the outlines of the face and limbs. He then encases the model in a mould, built of clay, as described in Chapter III. Before running in the molten metal into the mould, the mould is heated, thus causing the *moin* to ooze out of a hole left for that purpose. The metal is then run into the cavity thus formed, and when cool the mould is broken up and the casting taken out and polished in the usual way.

The first steps in the manufacture of a brass tray or salver of the Benares ornamental type is

(b) Engraving salvers, &c.

precisely similar to those adopted in making the ordinary *tháli* of everyday use, so that we need only take up the work at the stage, where ornamental process commences. After leaving the *siqligar* (or : *saiqalgar*, from Arabic, *salqal*—burnisher) or burnisher, the tray is passed on to the graver, who is technically known as the *naqqásnewala* (from Arabic, *naqqásh*—painter) or *chitr karnewálá* (from Sanskrit *Chitr*—delineation). His chief tools are the *karauna*, with which he traces the natural objects, such as trees and animals, which he wishes to engrave, and the *moti* and *gutrum*, a kind of punch, used for making round spots of larger or smaller size on the groundwork of the salver. The pattern traced, the salver is put on the fire and any unevennesses of its surface are removed with a wooden mallet. It is then passed on to the *tetóbwálá*, who dips it in *aquafortis* (*tazáb*) to remove its blackness and improve its colour. After this he washes it and passes it on to the *siqligar* for a final burnish. One of the commonest patterns is that known as *dúnewálá*. The cost price of a tray made of this pattern is Rs. 2-2-0 a ser. Another pattern is known as the *rukhd*. This design is traced with a pair of compasses, and takes its name from a peculiar kind of chisel, named *rukhd*, which is used for making the spots on the surface of the salver that give it such a fine finish. The cost price of the *rukhd* salver is Rs. 2-4-0 per seer, and it is calculated that one artisan alone working at a *rukhd* salver weighing a seer and a half would finish it in six days.

Ubhár kd kám—Or raised work (from *ubhár*—a swelling or rising) is the prettiest of all the ornamental processes for which Benares is famous. The plain salver is first fixed to a block of sealing wax (*láki*) in an inverted position, after which the design is marked with a pair of compasses and inked over, *litáná*. A hammer with a longish head rounded off at one end, termed a *got katkauri*, is used in order to raise the surface while the design is elaborated (*uscháá karuá*) with chisels of various shapes and sizes. Next, the clear spaces between the figures are levelled (*cháuras*) with the *cháursi*, a broad flat tool. The plate is now taken from the wax and placed on the fire, then taken off, cooled, and cleaned with sand and a solution of alum and tamarind. All undue elevations are corrected with the *got katkauri*, and the plate inverted is replaced on the wax block. The outlines of the figures are sharpened (*Kisdruá*) with a tool called the *golqalam*, and the figures themselves carefully finished off with a number of small fine tools. The plate is now again taken from the wax block and heated and any fissures or cracks are patched and repaired. It is then cleaned and passed on to the *teedbuálá*, and from him to the *sigligar*, who gives it a final polish.

A less expensive form of raised work is what is known as *zamín dabi kui ubhár*, which corresponds to our *basso relievo*. *Ganga jamni* is the name given to a kind of ornamental ware, in which a very beautiful effect is produced by the combined use of copper and brass or copper and bell-metal. Some very fine specimen of salvers of this description are to be met with in the *Thatheri bázár* though the meaningless profusion of gods and goddesses in the pattern rather offends against the canons of good taste.

There are numerous other ornamental processes that might be described did space allow, but the instances given above are sufficient to illustrate the far famed manufactures of Benares. The tools employed are even more numerous and varied than the patterns which they are employed to produce, so that an exhaustive inventory of them is quite out of the question.

Section 3.—The ornamental work done at Lucknow consists chiefly of beaten brass and copper *pándáns* and trays and *badáuds*. Some of these are of a very elaborate and intricate design, but the *modus operandi* is of the usual character and is merely an elaboration of the processes described in sections 18 and 20.

Section 4.—Idol-casting is the speciality of the Hamírpur district. This trade is limited to Srinagar in the Mahoba tahsíl and is carried on by a few families of Sonárs, who for some generations past have completely abandoned their proper occupation of goldsmith and adopted this business instead. The idols are of two kinds—solid and hollow. The method of making the first mentioned kind is exactly the same as that in vogue at Benares. A core of *main* is fashioned in the shape of the god: this is then coated with clay, the *main* is melted out through a hole left for that purpose, and the cavity filled in with molten metal. When cool the mould is broken and the idol is cleaned and polished. In making hollow idols a clay core is first fashioned in the shape of the god. This is then coated with a layer of *main* and an outer shell of clay is plastered on. The *main* is melted out and the resulting cavity filled up with brass. When cold the outer mould is broken up and the inner core is extracted by breaking up the burnt clay inside with a long nail. The hollow inside is then generally filled with lead, and a small brass cap, termed narya, is put out the hole at the top of the image. It might be supposed that this filling in the image with lead would occasion some difficulty at the time of sale, but in practice it does not, and Hindus do not generally, out of reverence, weigh their idols. The purchaser roughly satisfies himself of the amount and value of the brass contained in the idol.

Pure brass idols are sold at from Rs. 2 to Rs. 3 per ser, and those of which the interior is filled with lead at Re. 1-8 per ser.

Section 5.—The speciality of the Mathura district in the matter of brass and copper ware is the manufacture of small images of Hindu gods and chiefly of images of the infant Krishna. These are not made by Thatheras, but by men of the Sonár caste. The patterns are archaic and have certainly altered little since the beginning of the present century when many of them were figured in Moor's Pantheon. Small bowls, which by means of a syphon concealed within a cone rising from the centre of their bases, empty themselves when the liquid poured into them has reached a certain point, are made in several districts. The Mathura form of this toy is a brass bowl, which under the name of *bádeo katorá* has a fairly general reputation amongst the pilgrims from all parts of India who visit the Holy Land of Braj. On the top of the cone appears *Bádeo* or *Vasudeva*, carrying the infant Krishna, and the bowl empties itself, when the water within it rises to the feet of the child. It will be remembered that immediately after Krishna's birth Vasudeva carried Krishna across the Jumna from Mathura to Gokul, in order to save him from the massacre of the Innocents which had been ordered by the Hindu Herod Kansá. The Jumna was in flood, but on the feet of the holy child touching them the waters receded, leaving for Vasudeva a dry path across the river.

Section 6.—The extent of the outturn of these districts is very small. There is, however, a curious manufacture of brass animals of a rude description,

Jhánsi and Lalitpur.

used as toys by native children, and at Maraura, in tahsíl Makrani, there is a limited manufacture of genuinely artistic brass and bell-metal articles ranging in size from a large *degchi* to a small *lota*. The special feature of the Maraura work is the production of an incised pattern either in the casting or by subsequent engraving or by a combination of the two processes. This is afterwards filled up with copper and the whole turned and polished in a lathe. The price of a well finished article may be as high as Rs. 2 a ser.

Section 7.—In the Etáwah district there is small manufacture of ornamental articles, musical instruments, and sacrificial implements, which deserve some

Etáwah work.

notice. The work is carried on in a small town named Jaswantnagar, and the existence of such work at this place seems to have been unknown to Europeans till it was discovered last year by Mr. Dobbs, then Assistant Magistrate.

Candlesticks form one of the chief articles produced at this town. They are made in all sizes, from small light double-branched candlesticks up to magnificent candelabra of 50 branches, a specimen of which exists in one of the temples in the district. With the exception of the *parái* or tray on which the candlestick stands, all the rest is manufactured by casting in the manner described in section 7 of Chapter III, last method. The branches are adorned with various sorts of foliage and crocodile heads, the lines on the leaves (*naqqáshi*) being developed with a file after the casting is complete. The branches are known as *ddli*, the stem as *dari*, the pedestal as *cháaki*, and the sockets as *pidli*.

The musical instruments consist of marriage trumpets ; the *turái* and *kasdál* or *bhobu*. These are beaten from sheet brass into cylinder shape and then soldered.

The *kasdál* is much the larger of the two trumpets. Both are played by Dhánuks at marriage festivals, the *kasdál* emitting a long, sustained vibrating howl, while the *turái* produces two short, sharp notes. Among the sacrificial implements the most interesting, in spite of its hybrid name, is the *pujá ká gilás*. It contains almost all the implements necessary for worship and is used by Brahmans, both in private and in the temple. It is in shape like a glass with a top to it. This top is termed *ghantá* and can be rung as a bell during the time of worship, as it has a tongue (*lorki*) hung inside it. The *ghantá* fits into the *pánchpátr*, or vessel into which the priest pours water for the purpose of washing his hands and mouth before commencing worship. The next portion is the *gilás* used for holding water for the priest or idol's ablutions. The fourth portion is the *kopár* or saucer. Water is poured into this from the *gilás*, and the image of the god (*múrat*) is bathed therein. The remaining portions all fit into the *kopár*. They are, the *áchman* a little copper spoon, used by the priest for conveying water to his mouth ; the *shisha*, or small flat box, containing a minute mirror, in which the priest can contemplate his reflection after finishing his ablutions ; the *sompatti*, used for keeping grated red and white *chandan*, which the priest plasters on his forehead ; the *targalia*, a flat saucer for holding the rice with which the god is fed at the close of the *pujá*.

Section 8.—The vessel to be ornamented is covered entirely with *lac* and the pattern is traced on it with a pencil first and then with a steel pointed *galam*. After this the vessel is passed on to the *nichaiya* or graver, who engraves the pattern on the metal and then returns the vessel to the first workman, who fires the vessel and thus removes the coating of lac. After this it is given to a third man, who proceeds to colour it, and after beating the vessel slightly, coats it again with lacquer. Then with a tool termed *kaiya*, which also has to be heated, he rubs the surface of the vessel, thus removing all the lacquer except that which has run into the engraved pattern. All that now remains to be done is to clean the vessel. A powder (*manúri*) mixed with water is rubbed on the surface of the vessel with a piece of matting. This *manúri* is made of the burnt fragments of some old crucible. A second polish is given with *kuraud*, and finally the vessel is rubbed up with ashes by means of an old pudding cloth. This removes the blackness and oil, if any, which may have gathered on the surface of the vessel, and gives it a good finish. The only lacquer used is chhapra lac, which is coloured according to taste. There are no settled patterns, each workman evolving his own pattern out of his head as he proceeds.

Moradabad work.

Section 9.—This industry is one which is very widely carried on throughout the province, not only in big towns and manufacturing centres, but also in small villages. No one, even the most superficial observer, can have failed to be struck with the curious passion native women appear to have for decorating their arms and feet with trinkets : among the richer classes silver is the metal employed for this purpose, but the poorer classes have to content themselves with ornaments of bell-metal or some other alloy.

Woman's ornaments.

To commence with the ornaments worn on the arm.

The *mathia*.—This is a set of some 25 to 30 rings that are worn from just below the elbow up to the wrist. The whole set collectively and each ring separately is known as *mathia*, and the aggregate weight of the set is from 2½ to 3 sers. The largest ring fitting round just below the elbow is called the *pachhela*, the next one *majhua*, and the rest *agela*. A number of *pháil* rods are cast in an earthen mould, *kamchrá*, sufficiently long to make either one or two *mathid*. The rods, when cast, are beaten into the requisite thickness and are at this stage called *ddat*. They are then heated over a charcoal fire and beat into a round shape. After this they are filed and lathed in the usual manner and are ready for the market.

The *mathid* sells at the rate of Re. 1-4 per ser, the set for both hands costing from Rs. 2-3 to Rs. 4. They are generally manufactured from old metal.

The *dad*.—This is a bracelet worn about halfway up the forearm. It is confined to Ahírs and Chamárs.

The *chunwaka dahariyd* is a bracelet worn chiefly by Lodhis and Káchhis. It has an outer beading called *rabba* and inner indentation named *sút*.

The *naugari* is a bracelet consisting of little knobs of bell metal, cast into various rough shapes and strung together on a string.

The *ghunghard* is a bracelet consisting of a threaded row of small castings like miniature half opened oyster shells containing a little ball of iron, *kankar*, held captive inside. These castings are made in three pieces, *viz.*, the two valves of the shell (*topi*) and the tail pierced with a hole (*kuadla*), by means of which they are threaded together. They are worn chiefly by Ahírs, Lodhis, Káchhis, and Chamárs.

Anklets and *toe rings*.—The most important anklet worn is the *karri* or *kdrá* as it is called at Benares. The method of moulding these ornaments has been fully described under section 7, Chapter III, and need not be repeated here. The *karra* is extremely heavy, weighing from a quarter of a ser to a ser and quarter. In the Eastern Provinces of the North-Western Provinces and in Bengal even heavier ones are worn. *Karrás* are either round (*gol*) or six-sided (*palúiddr*) : sometimes they are plain (*sidá*), and sometimes chased (*naqqáshiddr*) *pátal. Karrás* sell at the rate of one rupee per ser and are made ordinarily from old metal. Nearly all women's ornaments made from *pháil* or *kaskut* are tinned before being worn. This is almost invariably the case with *karrds*. The reason given by the manufacturers is that heavy ornaments like *karrde*, &c., occasionally set up sores by friction: unless there was some protective medium, such as tinning, there would in such cases be great danger of blood poisoning from the copper that is present in the alloy.

Chhalld or *chhara*.—A thin light anklet. There are two kinds—one plain and the other with a kind of external 'dog tooth' ornament all the way round. *Chhalide* are usually sold in sets of three, the ornamental one being worn between the two plain ones. In Benares the name *chhullá* is given to toe rings.

Anautá or *anwat*.—This is a ring for the big toe and is of three kinds. First, we have the *ansula jhinjharidar*. The upper half of the ring which goes over the toe consists of a broad net work arch (*jhinjhari*), from the centre of which rises a crown *múrhá*. The lower semicircle of the ring is known as *torola*. From one side of the ring there projects a kind of tail (*naryá* or *dáúre*), which is placed between the second and third toes to keep the *anwat* in place.

(2) *Gol anwat*.—This has no network, but is ornamented with chasing (*naqqáshi*).

(3) *Lamba anwat*.—This has a peculiar crown (*murha*), with a spike (*nok*).

The *nohiya* and *bichiya* are small rings for the little toe, also decorated with crowns.

The *palwán* is a most elaborate ring, worn on the middle toe. Its feature is the *tdli*, which is fixed on the upper side of the ring. All round the edge of this are inserted small rings *laura*, on to which are strung minute metal knobs, *rond*, forming a kind of fringe all round the whole *palwán*. In the centre of the disc is fixed a crown or flower, *phúl*. Besides these elaborate rings, there are a number of quite plain toe rings called *puriya* and *chholla*, that are sold very cheaply in sets of Rs. 2-4-0.

Bracelets, anklets, and toe rings form the staple product of the brass and copper worker with regard to female ornaments; but at Benares, Ajodhya Sunárs make necklaces of *kansá* called *hansli*, and other small studs and trinkets are made in the various towns in the country.

Section 10.—Before leaving the subject of the ornamental work produced in the copper and brass trades of India, a word must be said as to the effect of foreign influence on Indian art. Sir George Birdwood, in his "Industrial Arts of India," has pointed out the danger of "interference in the direct art education of a people who already possess the tradition of a system of decoration founded on perfect principles, which they have learnt through centuries of practice to apply with unerring truth." But putting aside the question of direct art education, it cannot be said that western influence has even indirectly had a favourable influence on Indian Art. The ordinary western public is not sufficiently well educated in the principles of Indian Art to be able to distinguish between really good or merely showy patterns, and, provided it gets its money-worth of gods, wild beasts, and jungle, is generally content. The Indian artificer must cater for his market, and as the demand is brisk, cares little whether the pattern he turns out is of poor design and worse execution. In dealing with Benares and Moradabad work, mention had already been made of the unhappy transference of native decorative patterns to articles of purely European design and use. This kind of work will probably increase, with the growing popularization of English habits among natives. The present may be merely a period of transition and pure Indian art may yet see a revival, but there is no doubt that the market of to-day is unable to call forth from the modern Indian handicraftsman the same quality of design and workmanship that his father displayed in the days when the workman lived at his master's house and wrought his craft stimulated alternatively by fear of the lash and hope of large reward.

Foreign influence on native art.

GLOSSARY.

Note.—The brass and copper manufactures possess a fairly copious vocabulary of technical terms. Accuracy in transliteration has been aimed at, as far as possible, but any one who has ever attempted to carry on a conversation amid the deafening noise of a Thatheri Bazár will readily understand how easy it is to mistake the exact spelling of some new word or term that the enquirer has never heard before.

Hindustani.			Section and Chapter.		English.
			Section.	Chapter.	
A					
Anná	...	...	16	III	Open furnace.
B					
Baddhí	...	...	11	III	The strap used to pull the lathe.
Baghelí	...	...	11	III	A part of the lathe.
Bagís	...	...	17	III	The vertical side of a thálí.
Bál ...	...	...	16	III	A sledge hammer, cf. ghan.
Bálí ...	...	...	19	III	A pointed headed hammer.
Bánkas	...	...	4	I	A grass used for cleaning vessels.
Bamlí	...	...	8	III	An instrument for removing superfluous molten metal.
Bhángar	...	...	1	III	The worst kind of copper.
Bharat	...	...	2	III	Prince's metal; an alloy of zinc and copper, cf. kasbat.
Bhaṭṭí	...	...	9	III	A furnace.
Biswat	...	...	6	III	The soil from anthills. See balue mittí.
Boíí	...	...	8	III	A crucible, cf. ghariya.
Brihaspati	...	...	3	I	The god of gold.
Budh	...	...	3	I	The god of lead.
C					
Chák	...	...	11	III	A lathe.
Chaktí	...	...	13	III	A patch of metal, cf. fhfr.
Charakh	...	...	11	III	A lathe.
Chandan	...	...	7	IV	A kind of powder rubbed on the forehead.
Chaursí	...	...	3	IV	A broad, flat tool, used in raised work.
Chheni	...	...	18	III	A short, stout, handleless chisel.
Chitr karnewálá	...	...	3	IV	A graver (from Sanskrit chitr = delineation).
Chanákhá	...	...	17	III	A pair of compasses, cf. parkái.
D					
Dabká	...	...	9	III	The furnace in which metal is fused.
Dálí ...	...	...	7	IV	The branch of a candlestick.
Dánewálá	...	...	8	IV	A kind of decorative pattern.
Dántá	...	...	13	III	Dove-tailing (lit., a tooth).
Darí ...	...	...	7	IV	The stem of a candlestick.
Darj...	...	...	7	III	The crack between the upper and lower mould.
Daurí	...	...	4	I	A platter of leaves.
Dhálál	...	...	} 10	III	The pouring of the fused metal into the mould.
Dhardí	...	...			
Dharkál	...	...			
Dháilá	...	...	10	III	The workman who performs the above process.
Dhawha	...	...	9	III	See Dabka.
Dhaíá	...	...	17	III	Sloping side of a thálí.
Dhaunksi	...	...	9	III	Bellows, cf. khál.
Dhudhá	...	...	9	III	The ducts leading from the bellows to the furnace.
Diwálí	...	...	} 11	III	The strap used to pull the lathe, cf. baddhí.
Dálí	...	...			

10

Hindustani.			Section and Chapter.		English.
			Section.	Chapter.	
G					
Gabbá	...	...	7	III	The inner core of the mould.
Ganga jamni	...	...	3	IV	A term applied to articles made partly of one metal, partly of another.
Gehrá	...	...	16	III	A stone anvil.
Gerú	...	...	4	III	A kind of red earth.
Ghan	...	...	16	III	A sledge hammer, cf. Bál.
Gharat	...	...	15	III	Term applied to beating out old metal.
Ghariyá	...	...	6	III	A crucible cf. bota.
Golqalam	...	...	3	IV	A tool used in sharpening the outlines of figures in raised work.
Gulmuahá	...	...	9	III	Round headed, applied to hammers, &c.
Gurzóm	...	...	3	IV	A kind of punch.
Gulli	...	...	} 15	III	Cast plate of metal, cf. khatí.
Gurí	...	...			
H.					
Hárí	...	...	19	III	Concave anvil of stone, cf. okhli.
Hathaura	...	...	18	III	A hammer.
Hathaari gol	...	...	3	IV	A round-headed hammer used in Benares work.
I					
Imli	...	...	17	III	Tamarind.
Itwár or Samj	...	...	3	I	The god of copper.
J					
Jahází	...	...	1	IV	Fourth grade copper.
Jajhar	...	...	1	III	Second grade copper.
Jastá	...	...	1	III	Zinc.
Jatao	...	...	6	III	See káli mitti.
K					
Káiyá	...	...	5	IV	A tool used in Moradabad work.
Kajaaí	...	...	7	III	See khardani.
Kamothi	...	...	6	III	See under (Mitti káli).
Kánsá	...	...	} 3	III	Prince's metal: an alloy of zinc and copper cf. Bharat.
Kankut	...	...			
Kánsi	...	...	3	III	Bell-metal: an alloy of tin and copper cf. Phál.
Karauni	...	...	3	IV	A graving tool.
Karod	...	...	19	III	See Sardaij.
Kasaura	...	...	4	III	A rare kind of solder.
Katarná	...	...	17	III	A pair of clippers: a wooden groove in the anvil.
Kái	...	...	17	III	A pair of clippers.
Káib	...	...	16	III	A block of wood in which the anvil (Nehái, q. v.) is placed.
Kinárná	...	...	3	IV	To sharpen the outline of a figure.
Khál	...	...	} 9	III	Bellows, cf. Dhaukhni.
Khálí	...	...			
Kharád	...	...	11	III	A lathe, cf. kwad, &c.
Khardaní	...	...	7	III	An iron scraper used in lathing.
Kharwaj	...	...	11	III	A filer's tool made either of wood or iron.
Khas	...	...	4	III	A sweet smelling gram used for cleaning dishes.
Khinchwá	...	...	11	III	The work men who pulls the lathe strap.
Khunná	...	...	7	III	The peg supporting the lathe rod.
Khuil	...	...	15	III	A cast metal plate, cf. gulli.
Kothá or Kothá	...	...	6	III	A furnace.

Hindustani.	Section and Chapter.		English.
	Section.	Chapter.	
K—(continued).			
Kumharoti	6	III	See under *Miṭṭi kāli*.
Kūnch	16	III	A long rod or tweezers.
Kánd			
Kúnj	11	III	A lathe.
Kún			
Káng	11	IV	Corundum ; used for polishing vessels.
Kurund	8	III	A crucible, *cf. ghurya*.
Kuthálí			
L			
Labni	17	III	A chisel, *cf. rauda*.
Láhí	2	IV	Sealing wax, lac.
Likhná	2	IV	To ink over a pattern.
Lodhrá	1	III	Third grade copper.
M			
Main	2,4	IV	A mixture of wax and resin for moulding.
Mangal	9	I	The god of brass.
Manuri	8	III	A polishing powder.
Masturi			
Mamrhi	9	III	The furnace in which the metal is fused.
Mojhí ... ... —			
Maṭhan	19	III	A square-headed hammer.
Misijosh	4	III	Solder, *cf. ráaf*.
Miṭṭí			
—— Káli or chikní ...	6	III	A heavy dark clay=tank clay.
—— Pili			A light yellow clay.
—— Ilalui			Sandy earth.
Mohkár	20	III	The mouthpiece of a *pagrá*.
Mukhandá			
Mohlá	20	III	The upper half of a *pagra*.
Moti	2	IV	A graving tool.
Muhrá	7	III	The hole left in a mould for the entrance of the molten metal.
Maugari	17	III	A mallet or hammer.
Múnj	2	I	A grass used for cleaning dishes.
N			
Nák	11	III	A part of the lathe.
Námbái	4	I	A professional cook.
Nánd	17	III	A vat.
Naqqáshewálá ...	2	IV	A graver (from Arabic *Naqqash*=a painter).
Nariyá	4	IV	A small brass cap to cover the hole left in hollow idols.
Naushádar	4	III	Sal ammoniac.
Nihái	19	III	An anvil of iron.
O			
Okhli	19	III	See *Hári*.
P			
Pagrá or Págé	15	III	Small round earthen mould in which plates are cast.
Pallá	7	III	The outer shell of the mould.
Pán or Paná	16	III	Metal sheet beaten from a brass plate.
Parkár or Parkál ...	17	III	A pair of compasses, *cf. chandkhá*.
Palhawat	4	I	A grass used for cleansing vessels.
Pendi	17	III	The bottom of a vessel.
Pharuí	7, 11	III	A wooden support for the arm of the workman at the lathe.
Phúl	2	III	An alloy of copper and tin, *cf. Kánsi*. Bell-metal.
Pilla	7	IV	The socket of a candlestick.

Hindustani.		Section and Chapter.		English.
		Section.	Chapter.	
Q				
Qainchí	... ...	18	III	A pair of scissors.
R				
Rabu	... ...	3	I	The god of brass alloy.
Randá	... ...	11	III	A plane : a turning tool.
Rángá	... ...	1	III	Pewter : sometimes = tin.
Ránj	... ...	4	III	Solder, cf. misrfoch.
Raskapúr	... ...	4	III	Corrosive sublimate, used for colouring alloys.
Reh	... ...	2	I	Alkali, a purificator.
Retí	... ...	11	III	A file.
Mítín	... ...	11	III	A filer.
Rukhn	... ...	2	IV	A kind of chisel : also a decorative pattern named thereafter.
Rúsá	... ...	1	III	A good kind of copper (Russian ?), formerly imported into Benares.
S				
Sabrá	... ...	19	III	A vertical cone-shaped anvil.
Sabri	... ...	8, 19	III	A pointed instrument : as an anvil.
Sachhá karná	... ...	2	IV	Elaborate a design.
Sajji	... ...	4	III	A refuse salt, used as flux.
Sánchá	... ...	7	III	A mould.
Sandán	... ...	19	III	A kind of anvil.
Sánsí, Sánsí Sandasn, Sanrasn	... ... }	8	III	Tweezers.
Sari	... ...	3	I	The god of iron.
Saráng	... ...	19	III	A slanting anvil, resting on a wooden support (harod).
Sargá, Salgá, Salngá	...	7	III	Iron rod on which the mould revolves while being lathed.
Shámdán	... ...	19	III	A T-shaped anvil.
Siqligar	... ...	2	IV	A burnisher corr. from Persian saiqalgar = Arabic Saigal, a burnisher.
Sísa	... ...	1	III	Lead.
Sona	... ...	3	I	The god of silver.
Sudh	... ...	2	I	Ceremonially pure (cf. metals).
Sohágá	... ...	4	III	Borax : a flux.
Sukra	... ...	3	I	The god of pewter.
T				
Tánbá	... ...	1	III	Copper.
Tasma	... ...	11	III	The strap used to pull the lathe of Drwali.
Tezáb	... ...	2	IV	Aqua-fortis.
Thik	... ...	12	III	A patch of metal for mending, cf. chakti.
Tutrí	... ...	5	I	A spout.
U				
Ubhár ká kám	...	2	IV	Raised work, alto relievo (for ubhár = rising, swelling).
Ulchniyá	... ...	8	IV	A graver.
Z				
Zánfaráni	... ...	1	III	The best kind of copper.
Zamín dabháí ubhár	...	2	IV	Bas-relief.